THE SUMMERHOUSE GIRLS

M J HARDY

Copyrighted Material

Copyright © M J Hardy 2023

M J Hardy has asserted her rights under the Copyright, Designs and Patents Act 1988 to be identified as the Author of this work.

This book is a work of fiction and except in the case of historical fact, any resemblance to actual persons, living or dead, is purely coincidental.

All rights reserved. No part of this book may be reproduced or transmitted in any form without written permission of the author, except by a reviewer who may quote brief passages for review purposes only.

This book uses UK spelling

FOREWORD

'Jealousy is when you count someone else's blessings instead of your own.'

THE SUMMERHOUSE GIRLS

A friendship that took over thirty years to build and days to destroy.

This is the last day of my life.

I say that with certainty because of where I am now.

When I was a child I wrote a diary.

I never expected anyone would read it.

Fanciful childish nonsense, at least that's what I hoped they'd think.

Fast forward to the future and the last entry I made is the reason I'm standing at this grave, wondering if I'd still be here if I had never written that last damning paragraph.

I'm almost certain the answer would be no.

I thought I had friends. It turns out I was alone all the time.

A tale of friendship, secrets, and lies.

Betrayal and broken promises are the ingredients for the most delicious revenge.

1

CATHERINE

Sometimes friends can be a blessing, often a curse, and I can't decide which one applies to my current situation. I'm not even sure why I agree to this in the first place. I'm a wife and a mother with responsibilities. I'm no longer sweet sixteen with the world at my feet, eager to experience everything life throws at me, good things only, of course. Nobody wants the pain life sometimes dishes out like cold spaghetti and flat coke.

A disappointment that is hard to take sometimes, like rain on the first day of your holiday, or a flat tyre at daybreak when any passer-by is almost certainly a murderer.

The traffic on the way to the airport is interminable and

the conversation predictable, but despite my gloom I plaster a fake smile on my face and act as if I am excited to leave the cold February climate of home.

"It's busy today."

The gruff tones of my taxi driver point out the obvious as we join a queue of traffic exiting the slip road to the airport and, once again, I steal a glance at my watch and wonder if I'll have time to look around the duty free.

I wonder why it's always a cold grey morning when I leave the country and not much better when I return. Maybe one day I'll leave in full sunshine, but in the past thirty years or so that's never been the case. At least it feels that way.

The fog has lifted, which is a plus, and I hope it doesn't set our departure back at all.

"Where did you say you were going again?" The driver says with interest, and I mumble, "Dubai."

"On your own?"

"No, with friends."

"Are they meeting you there?" He enquires.

"Yes, it was easier that way."

I'm not sure it was, but as we all live in different parts of the country, I suppose it was the best plan.

"A girl's trip?"

I sigh, resigned to passing the time of day with the chatty driver.

"We met at school, what must be close to forty years ago now."

"That's impressive. I lost touch with my friends from school as soon as I left."

He chuckles as he cuts up a slow-moving motorist in front and as they sound their horn in anger, he shakes his head as if they were the one in the wrong.

"More accidents are caused by drivers who don't know

how to drive a car. Take that last one, for instance. Twenty under the speed limit and braking at every bend. I'm surprised I didn't hit the back of her."

"Her?"

I smile to myself because that driver was definitely a man.

"It's always a woman. They are cautious, worried about speed, and too nervous."

"It sounds as if you just described me."

I laugh softly, and he grins in the rear-view mirror.

"I disagree."

"Why?"

"Because you're travelling to a place most women would fear going to alone."

"I won't be alone."

"Ah yes, your friends. What's the occasion?"

"One of us is the first one to reach fifty, so we thought we'd celebrate."

"What happens when the rest of you catch up?"

"We reminisce about this trip over a glass of prosecco on a meal out one night."

"It sounds as if your friend is lucky to be the first. She gets the memory."

"She does. Then again, she always did."

Luckily, the traffic starts to move faster and ten minutes later we pull to a stop at the drop off area. It doesn't take long to exit the cab, tip the driver and wheel my case towards the departure terminal.

I shiver and pull my coat around me as the last icy fingers of air grasp at my skin. Maybe the fact it's thirty degrees at our destination made my decision for me because it's certainly no hardship leaving the cold winter behind.

I make my way to the check in area and try to dodge the plethora of travellers who appear to be walking around in a daze. I glance at my phone in the hope the others are here already, but so far only one message relays that fact.

GINNY

I'm here. I'll hover by check in zone C.

I head in that direction and wave at my friend Ginny with considerable relief that I'm not on my own anymore.

"Catherine, over here." She waves frantically and I quicken my pace, reaching her side with a huge smile on my face.

"Ginny, you look amazing."

"Same."

As always, my friend is dressed as if she's about to attend a business meeting and is wearing a smart navy trouser suit with a white t-shirt under a jacket that flares at the hips. Her smart matching leather bag is zipped tightly shut, unlike my own, which is bulging with last-minute additions that I forgot to pack.

Chaos follows me everywhere but has no place in Ginny's life, and I don't miss the glance of disapproval that she tries hard to disguise when she regards my appearance.

Unlike Ginny, I'm dressed for comfort and my leggings and baggy sweatshirt disguise my guilty pleasure for eating junk food. I've always been the same. If I wasn't finishing off my daughter Sally's food and snacks, I was bingeing between meals. My hatred of everything fitness means my skin has stretched to accommodate rather than remain toned and fat free. I understand Ginny's disappointment because nobody is more disappointed in me than myself.

"Have you heard from the others?" She enquires, and I shake my head.

"No."

"Me neither, although is that...?"

She begins to wave wildly and shouts, "Samantha, over here!"

I turn and a genuine smile lights my face when I see our friend racing across the concourse, looking agitated.

"I'm sorry I'm late guys. The traffic was insane."

"It's fine, but we should probably check in now. I mean, I haven't eaten yet and we're cutting it fine."

Ginny has always been the practical one, even at school, and morphed into the successful independent woman we all expected.

She is a top estate agent who never fell into the marriage trap like the rest of us and sometimes I really envy her that. She is confident, self-assured and sexually aware, always dating a different guy when we meet up and enjoying amazing holidays. She is never dull, and I live for her stories because compared to me, Ginny is living the dream and she knows it. She wouldn't have it any other way and as soon as her latest guy gets serious, she's onto the next one.

I wish I had a tiny shred of her confidence, but it appears she stole what was left when we queued in line.

We join the line for check in and it doesn't take long before we're airside and ordering a cooked breakfast to counteract the dreadful airline food they always serve in economy.

"Have you heard from the others yet?" Samantha enquires as she butters a slice of cold toast with frozen butter.

Ginny nods. "Amanda and Sonia flew out a couple of days ago. They decided to make a week of it and get some shopping in before the rest of us save their husbands from even more debt."

"At least they can afford it." I say quickly because out of all of us, they hit the jackpot with their husbands. Both of them making more money per week than the average person makes in a lifetime.

Samantha sighs. "It must be nice not to worry about the balance on the end of the credit card bill. To walk into a shop knowing that you can afford just about everything in there. My head spins with it all sometimes."

Ginny nods, a thoughtful expression on her face. "I could live like that. I *want* to live like that, but despite all my efforts, no city traders have swiped my profile on Tinder yet. Possibly I'm on the wrong dating app because all I get is guys who want sex and not a lot else."

Samantha laughs out loud. "And you're complaining about that."

We grin because Ginny is the most sexually active one of us and I know that as a fact because we make a point of discussing it at our monthly meetings.

It always surprises me how we've kept in touch all these years. Every month without fail, either in person at yet another restaurant surrounded by ice buckets of prosecco, or via zoom when we can't meet up in person. It's like a religion and none of us have deviated from the cause, which many think is impressive, and I suppose it is.

As we pay for our food, Ginny splits the bill three ways, and we all pay our share, as always. There are no favours and even if one of us has less, or something cheaper, we just divide it equally. It's why I drink so much when I'm with them because Sonia and Amanda get through at least a bottle each and the rest of us end up paying for it.

At first, it annoyed me because I'm careful with money and not because it's in short supply. My husband, Connor has his own business and has been very successful over the years. So much so I gave up my own dream of running a tea shop to work for him instead. I organise his paperwork and act as his assistant, which wasn't the best decision I ever made. Not that I made it in the first place, but my husband has a habit of making me feel bad for just about everything I do.

It was just easier to go along with his plan to keep as much of the profits in the family, not to mention keeping it away from the tax man and over the years he has run a tight ship, meaning I am forced to explain every single credit card transaction that appears on the statement, which usually results in a full-blown argument when he accuses me of overspending.

It's not as if we don't have the money, but he's a tight wad, which is probably why he's so successful.

We make our way to the gate and as we wait for the flight to board, Ginny turns to Samantha and says with interest, "How's business?"

Samantha runs a PR business that appears to be doing okay, which is just as well because her husband left her last year for a younger woman and she struggled to get over that. In fact, ever since it happened, she's a shadow of her former self and her business has been her saving grace.

"Good thanks." She appears a little edgy, which makes Ginny glance at me with concern, and I share it. Sammy always has kept her cards very close to her chest and we never really know what's going on in her world. She prefers to sit and listen rather than talk and I've noticed always manages to steer the conversation in a different direction if she is under the spotlight.

Luckily for her, the flight is called, and we make our way onto the plane and settle in a cramped row in economy for the next seven hours or so.

Ginny rolls her eyes when a woman with two small boys takes the row in front and almost immediately, the youngest one starts acting up. He kicks his chair, that appears to have a life of its own as it wobbles and bucks back and forth as he throws the loudest tantrum.

The mother starts yelling and the second boy starts coughing, causing the Japanese couple across the aisle to hold their face masks on more securely.

Samantha sighs and Ginny huffs with exasperation as the doors close, leaving us trapped with the family from hell in front of us.

Once airborne, I lean back in my aisle seat and close my eyes. It was an early start and I'm exhausted already. Ginny has extracted some noise cancellation headphones from her luggage and is typing on her MacBook Air and Samantha pulls out her kindle and shuts the whole world out as she loses herself in the pages of her latest romance.

As we head towards our destination, I am reminded once again of how unfair life can be. Sonia and Amanda flew out business class and were plied with alcohol and enjoyed luxurious seats. No doubt there wasn't a child in sight either. How the other half live and the other half want to and right at this moment, I'm one of them.

2

CATHERINE

DUBAI

After an arduous taxi ride, we reach our destination, and I am transported to another world. It's almost as if the air changes when we step from the cab. Purer somehow. The oxygen appears filtered to give the guest the full relaxing experience and the way the man waiting charges forward to help with our suitcases makes me believe I'm important for once in my life.

"Wow! This place is amazing already." Samantha says in awe as she gazes around at what can only be described as a palace.

I agree it's certainly impressive and Ginny gazes around with a keen interest, no doubt searching for the smallest flaw to complain about, to get us some sort of freebie.

"It's ok, I guess. I would have preferred to stay at that new one they opened last week with the light show and Beyoncé concert."

I share a look with Samantha, and we disguise our imminent eye rolls. For some reason, Ginny is never happy and always looks for the flaw in every plan, and it's become the part of her over the years that we are resigned to. A complaint always follows every meal, from cold food and undercooked meat to bad service and rude staff. At first it was embarrassing but we are so used to it now, it's a surprise when she remains quiet, and we don't have to look away with embarrassment when she steps on her high horse.

However, this place is impressive, and I doubt she can find one fault with it and as we head to reception, I'm interested to see if the rooms live up to first impressions.

I am pleasantly surprised because we are shown to three rooms overlooking the ocean that I would be happy to live in full time. They are all adjacent to one another and we meet on our respective balconies and gaze around with excitement.

"Wow! Sonia certainly knows how to travel five stars." I say in awe and Ginny replies slightly spitefully. "Well, she's had enough practice, I suppose."

"Have you heard from them yet?" Samantha enquires, and Ginny shakes her head.

"No. I texted her but never heard back. I'm sure she'll be in touch soon, though. Maybe we should unpack and then head to the bar. That's probably where they are, anyway."

Samantha nods in agreement. "You're probably right. I wish this place was all-inclusive, though."

"Me too." I nod because knowing how much my friends drink and imagining the prices this place must charge, it's doubtful most of us can afford the prices, anyway.

I leave my friends to it and head into my room, taking a moment to explore a place I'm alone in for once. It seems wrong that I'm excited about that. Aside from the nights Connor spends away on business, we have been together most of the time. Occasionally, he takes a holiday with his golfing friends and sometimes business is extended, sometimes for several weeks. But I haven't ever had a girl's holiday before and I'm a little on edge about that. It seems wrong somehow, as if the stars have shifted out of line, and I need to readjust.

Our daughter Sally attends boarding school. Something I wasn't happy to agree to, but Connor insisted. He told me she would get the best education that way and learn independence. It still feels wrong saying a tearful goodbye every term and counting down the days until the next break.

However, I'm here now with a determination to enjoy every minute of the surprise break that Amanda arranged for Sonia's fiftieth. We left it all in her capable hands because she insisted. All we had to do was book our flights and they would bulk book our accommodation. Sonia's husband runs the hedge fund for a property company, and they assured him of a discount. I'm a little nervous about it now that we're here because I'm almost certain this place didn't come cheap, discounts and all.

As I wander around exploring my home for the next few days, I desperately try to banish any guilt I may have brought with me.

I take a long luxurious shower in the largest bathroom I have ever seen and then pull on a maxi dress and brush my hair, making me feel instantly better as I wash away the fatigue of travel.

A loud knock on the door comes at exactly the right time and as I open it, I notice Ginny and Samantha are waiting in similar attire to mine.

"Sonia called." Ginny says, "They're waiting at the beach bar."

As I follow them along the impressive hallway, Samantha says with a touch of reverence.

"This place is amazing. I'm a little worried about how much it will cost, though."

Ginny shrugs. "Amanda assured us it would be within our budget and if it's too much, she will pick up the shortfall. Mind you, it's not as if she can't afford it."

I glance uneasily at Samantha, who shifts awkwardly on her feet because Ginny expects Amanda to always step in. It never sits well with me though, because surely her money is her own business and just because she has more of it than all of us, it doesn't mean we are entitled to it in any way.

As we make our way through a virtual palace, I am itching to take photographs of every Instagram worthy shot in sight. From the gold mouldings on the ceilings, to the sparkling chandeliers that are just about everywhere. The velvet covered chairs and impressive flower arrangements that are on every surface possible. This is luxury on a grand scale, and I am so unworthy as we pass through the opulence that we will call home for the next five days.

We head through the door into the sunlight, which almost blinds me after the gentle lighting of the interior. The heat hits me first and I sigh inside. This is what I came for. Leaving the British winter behind was no hardship and as I spy the turquoise sea stretching before me like a mirage, I thank my friends for insisting we make this a trip to remember.

When Sonia first suggested it at one of our monthly dinners, I was a little surprised and never really thought it would happen at all. Yet here we are now, and all the months of planning and expectation are about to be enjoyed and I intend on making the most of it.

3
CATHERINE

As we approach, the squeals from our friends greet us as Sonia and Amanda jump up from their seats, a vision in their flowing chiffon maxi dresses and floppy hats. Wealth obviously suits them. It always has, and I try to fight back the tinge of jealousy that always rears its ugly head when I'm around them.

"Catherine, you look amazing."

Sonia pulls me in for a hug and I return the compliment.

Amanda is next, and she smiles. "I'm so happy you agreed to come. Is Connor ok about it?" she says with concern, and I say brightly, "He's fine about it."

"Are you sure?"

"Yes, it's fine. It will do him good to fend for himself for a few days."

"I thought the same." She laughs as she references her own husband and then rolls her eyes. "Although he'll be buried in the Financial Times for most of it without me around to distract him."

She shakes her head. "It wouldn't surprise me if he sleeps on his office floor and orders his assistant to keep him supplied with food."

"What about the kids?" I reference her son and two daughters, who, despite attending the most expensive private schools, managed to swerve boarding and return home every night in Amanda's customised Range Rover.

"It's fine. My parents have moved in, which is probably why Jasper will stay at the office."

She laughs infectiously. "He hates all the fussing; you see, my mum takes it upon herself to treat him like one of the kids and he gets no alone time, and we all know how much of that he needs."

I smile because she's right about that. Jasper is alone in a crowd, always deep in contemplation or hiding behind the newspaper. He's a great guy, very personable and yet also extremely private, preferring his kids' company when we're all together than chatting with the husbands of my friends. The fact Connor always makes a beeline for him is embarrassing because I can tell Jasper is just being polite while he discusses never ending business with him, with a sense of self-importance that's embarrassing at times.

"How's your room?" Amanda enquires, with a worried frown, and I reassure her with a bright smile. "It's amazing. I've never stayed anywhere as palatial as this and, to be honest, I'm a little worried its above my budget."

Amanda shakes her head and smiles reassuringly. "Don't

worry, we got a great discount, and it will be no more than the usual four star, half board package from most tour operators."

As she reassures me, I can't help feeling relieved and I turn to Sonia as she interrupts our conversation. "You should see our suite. I have the most amazing friend in the world looking after me."

Amanda smiles as Sonia says with excitement, "We have two bedrooms in a suite that the King would be happy in. Both have king-sized beds, and a small living room connects them. We have our own bathrooms, and quite honestly, I never want to leave because the fabulous views of the ocean are the best I've ever seen."

Ginny appears green with envy as she shares a look with Samantha, who merely smiles with interest as Sonia brags about how much better her room is than ours.

If anything, Amanda appears embarrassed and, with a wave of her hand, says quickly, "Anyway, what would you like to drink? We have a bottle of prosecco in the ice bucket, or they do some mean cocktails that I've never seen the like of before."

"Ooh, a cocktail please." Samantha says with delight and Ginny nods. "Me too. It's the only time I bother when I'm abroad."

I nod with a grateful smile. "That sounds lovely, thank you."

As we settle down and Amanda hands us the menu, I listen to their chatter, preferring to take a back seat as always. Maybe it's because I don't believe my life is as interesting as theirs, or it could be because I'm used to listening rather than talking because nobody ever listens to me, anyway.

Sonia is full of her own importance as always and commands

everyone's attention as she regales us with stories of their flight and their stay in the first-class lounge. To be honest, it's all a world away from what I'm used to, and I can't really get excited about something that I'll probably never experience first-hand.

Ginny hangs on every word though and when Sonia stops, presses for more information with a hunger that doesn't escape me. I suppose she's always been impressed by wealth and works so hard to achieve it for herself and I must admire her for that because at least she wants to earn it, unlike my friends who married it.

Amanda is quiet beside me and as Sonia orders another bottle of prosecco, she whispers, "This is going to be a long night."

She grins as I laugh softly. "At least we all have our own rooms. Watch that mini bar in yours."

Amanda nods and stares at our mutual friend with a sad expression that surprises me. It's as if she has the weight of the world on her shoulders, but before I can ask about that, Sonia yells, "Come on guys, we're here to party. Let's order some more cocktails. It's not every day a woman turns fifty you know, and you're not far behind me."

Her hand shakes as she lifts her glass and slurs, "Life begins at fifty and I'm making the most of mine."

We raise our glasses and toast our friend and for some reason I cast my mind back on our school days and whisper to Amanda, "I can't believe we are still friends. To be honest, I never really thought we would make it this far."

Amanda nods. "It's strange but you are the only friends I kept in contact with outside the school run mums who I still catch up with from time to time, but this is, well, it's like family, I suppose."

Sonia catches our conversation and raising her glass, says

loudly, "To us. Our own special family and I just want to thank you all for being so incredible."

Amanda whispers, "Now I know she's had too much to drink."

The others laugh and to anyone looking in, they would see a bunch of women living their best lives. I almost wish that was the case, but appearances can be deceptive because one of us most definitely isn't.

4
CATHERINE

After a boozy welcome party, we all retire to our rooms to shower and change for dinner, and I take the chance to call home. Connor answers almost immediately.

"Hey, babe. I see you made it, ok."

"Yes. I had a good flight."

"I see."

He sounds distracted, which isn't unusual because Connor always has one ear on the conversation and the other on business.

"Have you heard from Sally?"

I'm eager for news about our daughter, knowing she always phones home around seven and Connor sighs.

"Yes. She's fine. Stop fussing around after her. She needs to be independent."

"She's fifteen years old, Connor. She's hardly an adult."

"Not far off, though. You really smother her, Catherine, which isn't doing any of us any favours."

"Smother her!"

I'm incensed because since when did parenting a child amount to smothering.

"How can I smother her when she doesn't even live with us?"

"Now you're getting emotional, and I can't deal with you when you've had a drink. You really should control your intake; I don't like what alcohol does to your mind."

He says with an aggression that makes me glad I'm not in the same room because when Connor gets angry, it doesn't end well for me.

The tears prick behind my eyes as I face up to my harsh reality. I fell out of love with my husband a long time ago and I'm even questioning if I ever loved him at all. They say absence makes the heart grow fonder. Well, good for them because absence is just highlighting what I don't have. Freedom.

As if to reinforce that, he says impatiently, *"Where did you put the Atkins file? I've been hunting for it all afternoon."*

"Have you tried the filing cabinet under A."

"Obviously."

He huffs and then says gruffly, *"Wait a minute."*

He puts the phone on speaker, and I hear him crossing the room and the sound of drawers opening and banging closed. Then he heads back and says angrily, *"You're losing it, Cathy. I found it next to Barnes and Greengage."*

I take a deep breath and count to ten because fire me for putting it in the B section by mistake.

Connor growls. *"Maybe I should hire a temp to get things back in order. I don't know why you can't perform even the simplest task these days. Are you hitting the menopause or something?"*

My mind is exploding with ways to kill him and make it slow and painful right now and I hiss, "I've got to go, somebody's at the door."

I cut the call before he can even answer and hurl my phone across the room in a fit of rage.

The fucking menopause. Is he kidding me? I couldn't hate him more right now if I tried.

My heart is thumping, and my blood is boiling because I am fast concluding that my husband is rapidly approaching his use by date.

It takes me a while to calm down, which is only achieved by a long hot shower and switching my mind onto other things. It's always the same. I argue with Connor and then focus on my friend's lives rather than my own car crash. I try to picture myself in their shoes. How amazing it must be to have it all! Wealth equals happiness in my book because my friends who have a lot of cash appear happier than me. Sonia and Amanda live dream lives. Doted on by their husbands and enjoying a happy healthy relationship with their children. I don't believe I've ever heard them mention any worries in the past thirty or so years, not life-changing ones, anyway.

Samantha had her fair share of problems over the years, mainly a husband with a wandering eye. However, even before she discovered his duplicity, it was apparent to everyone how much he doted on her. Just not exclusive, as it turned out.

Her PR business appears to be doing well, and she never complains. The fact she has no children is sometimes a blessing because she has nothing to tie her down or worry about. Of all of us, Samantha appears the happiest and I'm guessing that comes with freedom. Something that is becoming increasingly attractive to me.

My thoughts turn to Ginny, which makes me smile. Now there's a woman I admire. She appears to have life worked out and her independence is like a tempting treat in the bakery window. I want it so badly but know it's out of my reach because if I indulged it would be extremely bad for me.

I spy my phone on the floor in the corner where it fell, and an idea hits me that I immediately dismiss.

As I move to retrieve it, the idea grows even larger until it's standing before me and impossible to ignore.

I feel a sudden rush of excitement as I contemplate my idea and turn it around in my mind, expecting it to leave as quickly as it came.

I stare at the phone, not daring to believe it may be an option and as I wander onto the balcony with the phone still in my hand, I settle down on the chair and gaze out on the land of opportunity and change.

Why not? I'm my own person. At least I was once. I shouldn't be afraid of changing my own future and making my own decisions. This may well be the making of Catherine Bailey and I just need to grab some balls from somewhere and make it happen.

Once again, I glance down at my phone and my finger hovers over the App store. Nobody ever needs to know. I could live a secret life; an amazing life and nobody would ever find out.

My heart starts thumping and my mind begins to race as an idea consumes me that may turn out to be an extremely bad one.

5
SAMANTHA

I'm in love with this place. It's paradise on earth and has a mysterious edge I love and takes my breath away.

I love being here with the girls. The excited hum of conversation as we all catch up fills me with joy and I can't remember the last time my life felt so full. Since Ben left the house is incredibly lonely and despite business being good, it's lonely working by myself for most of the time with only my clients an email away.

I play badminton twice a week and go to the gym, but most of the time it's only me which is strange. That's why I've been looking forward to this trip so much because I get to spend it with the only people in my life who have always been there for me.

My friends.

Casting my mind back, I remember our days at Summerhouse fondly. We were a tight group. Maybe not as tight as we became, but it was good to be part of a family of sorts. As an only child, I never really had anyone to gossip with until I met the Summerhouse girls, as we called ourselves.

I loved being part of that. Included in a club with very exclusive membership. Part of the elite. At least I thought so. Sonia was popular and respected by our fellow pupils and teachers alike. She could do no wrong and was an authority figure that many wanted to emanate, me included. I was honoured to be included in her inner circle and have always been a little in awe of her.

If I could be like any of my friends, it would be Sonia and I'd do anything for her at all. That's why I jumped at the chance to join them on this trip, and I suppose my hero worship may be considered a little creepy to some. Then again, she deserves my undying loyalty because of what I did.

The shame flutters inside me, reminding me it will never go away. I will never be free. It's the chain around my soul dragging me down and ensuring my mistake will live with me forever.

I try not to think about it and push it to the back of my mind but in silent moments when I head back down memory lane, it's waiting to greet me with a wicked smile and a shake of the head, waving an admonishing finger at me and reminding me how despicable I am.

I head out onto the balcony and take in deep breaths of invigorating air. On the way from the airport the taxi driver told us they fabricate clouds in Dubai to bring the desert temperature down. It struck me as astonishing that man would be so bold as to take over from mother nature, but it obviously works for them because they have made the desert into a land of commerce, tourism, and wealth. I heard the oil was running dry, and they needed a new income stream, which is why they've relaxed the rules and encouraged the west to come east. I'm not complaining because this place is immeasurable and part of me wonders what it would be like to live here full time.

Many people make it their home. I know of many friends who took a bite of the apple, tempted by tax free cash and year-round sunshine. There is nothing stopping me from moving here and indulging in a brave new life, something Samantha Castle would never contemplate in a million years.

The idea has been brewing for some time. I understand I need a change, but is this it?

A tap on the door takes my attention and as I answer it, Ginny rushes past me like the whirlwind she is and says quickly, "What do you think of this place, Sammy?"

She casts a critical eye around my room and from the disappointment reflecting at me, I can tell my room is better than hers.

Ginny always wants the best of everything and hates it when someone else has better, and I bite back my smile and say happily, "I love it. Who wouldn't love paradise."

"If you say so," Ginny grumbles and heads out onto my balcony and gazes at the view with a slightly wistful expression on her face.

"What is it, Ginny?" I can tell something is on her mind and she sighs with a slight shrug of her shoulders.

"Do you ever get jealous, Sammy?"

I'm surprised by her question because I never thought Ginny was jealous of anyone. She has no reason to be, surely.

"Of course." I lean on the balustrade beside my friend and

gaze out on the same view, loving how the warm sun heats my blood and rests on my skin like the most delicious cashmere.

"It's not a nice feeling, is it?" Ginny sighs and I shake my head. "Not really, but that's all it is — a feeling."

I rest my hand around her shoulders in a comfort she obviously needs and say softly, "What is it?"

"I don't know. I work so hard. I always have and yet don't have much to show for it."

"You do."

I'm surprised and say reassuringly. "You own your home, have amazing things and enjoy no debts with a black book many would be envious of."

"But I'm still alone and nobody really cares about me." She appears dejected and I say sympathetically, "What's brought this on?"

She shrugs. "Please don't tell anyone. I'm confiding in you because you're probably the only one who can relate to my situation, but it's just that, well..."

She turns and smiles almost apologetically. "I'm lonely, Sammy."

I make to speak but she interrupts. "The guys I date are only after one thing, and I don't trust any of them. Sure, I've had a few keepers, but they didn't really measure up."

"In what way?" I always thought Ginny met some amazing guys who appeared genuine, and she shrugs, gazing wistfully over the skyline.

"They were ok but not really what I was looking for. I mean, not rich enough, I guess, with no direction."

She smiles guiltily. "I sound like a right bitch, don't I? The trouble is, when I see Sonia and Amanda and the life they lead, I want the same."

"I see." I feel a little sorry for Ginny because I never

thought she was jealous of our friends, and she huffs. "Who wouldn't want what they have? A rich adoring husband who funds a lifestyle many only dream about. No financial worries and everything they want a credit card swipe away, with none of the concerns of the bill."

"It does sound idyllic." I must agree with her because who wouldn't want that?

She sighs and gazes across the view where a modern city meets a man-made island, the stretch of water between separating leisure from commerce.

"Have you ever wanted to relocate?" I say on impulse.

"You know, change your life drastically in the hope something better is out there."

Ginny says with surprise. "What do you mean?"

"This place."

I wave my hand at a vista that is nothing like the one I usually enjoy.

"Dubai has a thriving ex-pat community. There are endless opportunities, cash free money and year-round sunshine."

Ginny nods, her eyes sparkling with the same idea I have, and she smiles. "I've never considered it, but now you mention it, it could be interesting."

I nod, a shiver of excitement rippling through me as my idea takes root.

"What if we joined forces and moved our businesses here?"

My enthusiasm takes over as the idea runs away with me.

"You could sell property here and I can work anywhere. My clients are via email, anyway, and I'm sure I'd get many more over here. We could share an apartment and make a new life. What do you think?"

Ginny rewards me with a huge smile and her eyes flash as my idea extends to incorporate her.

"You know what, Sammy, you may be onto something."

She gazes out at the view, and I can almost hear her mind working from here and then as she turns, I'm astonished at the tears glistening in her eyes.

"Thank you."

I'm a little confused, and she leans forward and grasps my hand in hers.

"You have a habit of making the world a better place, Sammy. You always have, and we really should explore this idea of yours."

We share a look and it's as if we have been travelling on different paths and met at a junction. Will we continue the journey together, or will it just be a brief chat at the crossroads before we end up walking in different directions?

It will be interesting to find out.

6

SAMANTHA

We meet at the bar later and, as always, Sonia and Amanda are knee deep in prosecco already.

"Sammy, over here." Sonia waves from across the room and I smile as I head over.

"This place is amazing."

Sonia nods. "It sure is. Amanda told me Jasper brought her here for their anniversary and I was keen to experience the magic for myself."

Amanda nods, but something in her expression startles me. She appears a little upset if I'm honest, but as I catch her eye, she smiles and drops a quick wink before saying brightly, "It's the perfect place to celebrate reaching half a century."

"I'm not sure I like that description." Sonia says in horror. "You know, fifty is the new thirty, in my book, anyway, and I intend on making the most of the rest of the years I have left."

Amanda nods and raises her glass. "I'll toast to that."

Ginny and Catherine make their way across the room and I smile at Ginny, hoping that our conversation earlier will turn into a lot more than just words.

She flashes me a conspiratorial smile and takes the seat beside me.

Amanda hands out more prosecco and as we raise our glasses, she says warmly, "To Sonia and to friendship. Long friendships at that and let's hope the next fifty years are equally amazing."

We echo the toast and as we take a moment to drain them, I'm a little disturbed to witness the slight shake of Sonia's hand as she sets it down on the table.

As the conversation flows, so does the alcohol, and I'm worried that the bill at the end of the evening will be more than I can afford. It's difficult to monitor because we agreed to divide the final total equally, as we always do, which is fine for a night out, but a few days away in an expensive hotel is a different thing entirely.

I'm not sure why but there's a strange atmosphere and I put it down to lack of sleep and the jet lag. It's almost as if a storm is building and we're at the centre of it, but as I glance around at my friends anyone else would say I was being ridiculous.

"I'd love to see your room." Catherine pipes up and Sonia nods, her face breaking out into a smug smile.

"I'll show you if you like."

"What now?"

I'm surprised and Sonia shrugs. "I need a wee, anyway. Why not now?"

They stand and, as tempting as it is to go and look, I stay with Amanda as Ginny and Catherine jump up to follow her.

As they leave the bar, Amanda sighs.

"Is everything ok?" I say with concern, and she shakes her head looking worried.

"I don't know. Sonia was a little quiet on the way out here and wasn't her usual bubbly self and when I asked if anything was wrong, she was quite abrupt."

"Do you think there's something wrong?"

Amanda nods. "It's definitely out of character. Do you think it's serious? I mean, it must be if she won't talk about it."

"I agree. Perhaps it has something to do with Daniel or the boys?"

Sonia and Daniel have two boys of an impressionable age who have been known to go off the rails occasionally.

Amanda nods. "I'm not sure, but Jasper told me he heard that Daniel's company is restructuring. His job may be at risk."

"Again." I'm amazed because this is definitely not the first time Daniel has lost his position and every time he managed to find another one with ease.

"Maybe that's why she's struggling." Amanda says thoughtfully. "I mean, she's always been a drinker, but nothing like she's been since we checked in. She drank a bottle of prosecco in the airport lounge even though it was six am."

She fixes me with a worried frown.

"I tried to ask, but she ignored the question and just took full advantage of the free bar on the plane and then fell asleep before landing."

"She could be drinking to dull the pain of whatever is worrying her?"

Amanda shrugs. "I guess, although it could be because Thomas got into a fight at school and was excluded for a week."

"Wow, when did that happen?"

"Two weeks ago. Sonia told me she was called in along with the other boy's parents and, by all accounts, Thomas has become quite the bully."

I bite my tongue because Daniel himself is a little bullish and I wonder if his son takes after him.

Amanda sighs. "Freddie has never liked him."

Freddie is her son who is around the same age as Thomas. They go to different schools, but as their families are close, they are more like brothers than friends.

"Since when? I always thought they got along well."

I'm confused, and Amanda shakes her head. "Not really. Freddie gets on better with Jamie, who told him that Thomas had been bullying this boy all term. The day in question, he reacted and hit back, which is why it came to the attention of the school. Normally he did it out of sight and the boy was so afraid he never said anything."

She shakes her head with disapproval. "I'm guessing that's the reason why Sonia's anxious. If it happens again, he will be excluded completely, and it will sabotage his final exams."

"Poor Sonia." I feel so sorry for her, and Amanda nods.

"It must be such a worry, but she'll pull through. They all will. On the way over, she told me they were planning a family holiday to Fiji in the Summer so things can't be all bad."

"Fiji! That's amazing."

I'm surprised at the bitterness in Amanda's eyes that she tries to disguise with a smile.

"Yes, the whole family is going on an all-inclusive trip of a lifetime."

"Lucky them." I say enviously and as the others return, I note the expression on Ginny's face, which tells me their room is every bit as luxurious as Sonia said it was and my heart sinks. Ginny's jealously is becoming a huge problem – for her, anyway, because she's letting it eat away at her and cloud her mind.

Catherine grabs another glass of prosecco and says to me, "You should see their room, Sammy. How the other half live. It's like a small palace within a palace."

"Speaking of which." We look up as Sonia says loudly, "Because we have a suite, we are granted access to the exclusive Raffles bar, otherwise known as the palace within a palace. You gain access via your room key in a special elevator to a private place only a select few gets to enjoy."

My heart sinks at the expression on Ginny's face as her eyes flash with jealously, and I'm grateful when Amanda says quickly, "We've arranged for three passes this evening for you as our guests. It involved a small fee, but it's worth it, just you wait."

She nods to Sonia, who claps her hands with excitement.

"Let's go and set up camp there instead. You should see the view."

As she stands, I note the half empty bottle of prosecco and say quickly, "Shall we bring this?"

Sonia shakes her head. "God no. We'll get one there. What would people think if we tumbled out of the lift holding a half empty bottle of plonk like a hobo?"

Her words crush me as they always have a habit of doing and as she turns away, Amanda whispers, "Take no notice of her. It's a great idea. I'll slip it into my bag, and nobody will know."

She does as she says with a conspiratorial wink and links her arm in mine.

"Come on, Sonia's right, the view is amazing, and we thought it would be a lovely treat on the first day of our trip."

As we head after our friends, I try to push down the inferiority complex that always follows me into these situations and shake the awkward vibes away. I should try to forget my worries and my life back home and just dive, with no inhibitions, into five-star luxury while it's here.

7
GINNY

I knew this was going to be a struggle. I'm not sure why, but it's becoming increasingly difficult for me to enjoy spending time with my friends. I'm not even sure when it began. It crept up on me one day when my attention was elsewhere and hasn't left.

My jealously is eating me up inside and it appears that I'm jealous of them all as a collective. Sonia and Amanda for their millionaire lifestyle, handed to them along with an engagement ring and a no expenses spared wedding.

Catherine has a husband and a daughter and doesn't worry about money at all. She works with her husband, so doesn't have the same nine to five commute that I have endured since leaving school. Then there's Samantha. She met an amazing soldier, the kind they write about in romance novels. Strong, brave and drop dead gorgeous, who I thought only had eyes for my friend. As it turned out, I was wrong about that, but he left her the house and her business is doing well, so she never worries about anything.

When she mentioned relocating to Dubai, I jumped at the opportunity. This could be the making of me. Surely, the opportunities are far-reaching here, and I may even bag myself my own rich husband and lead the life I've always craved.

I watch my friends as they giggle in the lift that is propelling us to exclusivity, and my hunger only increases with every level we pass.

I want this.

I want the dream and I won't rest until it's my reality.

The lift stops and opens into a space that takes my breath away. It's huge, light-filled and dripping with modern lighting like shards from a cave of stalactites.

A beautiful woman is playing a saxophone, and the soulful haunting melody caresses my senses and brings a smile to my face.

We walk into the room, and I note how quiet it is here. None of the rush of the masses, just a select group of people enjoying pre-dinner drinks with a buffet of appetisers that is free for the elite few.

Sonia says loudly, making me cringe a little, "Let's go to the rooftop terrace. You should see the view. It's spectacular."

We follow her through the double doors and step out into the dusky air, the candles flickering in the breeze as they sit on white covered tables set around a patio that overlooks the skyline.

We take our seats, and a waiter appears as if by magic

with a cocktail menu and my heart sinks. More drinks. How much will this all cost? Again, I feel envious of my friends who take the swipe of their credit card for granted, knowing they won't be saddled with the bill at the end.

Samantha gazes around in awe. "Wow, this is amazing. I could live like this."

Amanda nods. "I loved it when I visited with Jasper. I hoped you would too."

Sonia grins. "Well, make the most of it ladies, reality is a plane ride away and we don't have many days to enjoy this paradise."

Amanda nods. "Back to February. That's not a nice thought."

Sonia laughs. "I told Daniel we should cancel February every year and book a villa somewhere hot. You'd be up for that, wouldn't you, Amanda?"

I'm not sure if it's my imagination, but Amanda's expression says she's definitely not up for that, before she replaces it with a small polite smile.

"Of course. Who wouldn't?"

Sammy nods. "Actually…" She glances at me and grins. "I'm considering relocating here, and I've asked Ginny if she fancies sharing an apartment."

It's as if she's tossed a grenade into the room because my friends stare at her in shock before swinging their gazes in my direction.

"It's true." I shrug. "Samantha had the idea earlier today and as we both have no ties back at home. It makes perfect sense."

"But you've only just got here. It's a little rash, don't you think?" Catherine exclaims incredulously, and I laugh softly. "That's why it's so good to be us. Isn't that right, Sammy?"

She nods and says excitedly, "Think about it. We can work

here; my business will travel well, and Ginny could find a job with a property company out here. It's such an up-and-coming place and as we are all painfully aware, none of us are getting any younger, so why not seize the moment and run with it?"

Amanda laughs out loud. "It's an excellent idea. Good for you."

She turns to Sonia. "This is something Daniel would be interested in."

"What makes you say that?" Sonia says sharply, causing me to peer at her a little closer.

Amanda shrugs. "I thought he was into property developing. Perhaps he could throw some connections Ginny and Samantha's way."

For some reason, the conversation stills, and I'm surprised to see the frown on Sonia's face and Catherine appears a little nauseous.

I glance at Samantha, who appears as mystified as I am, and then the waiter returns with our order, and we fall on the brightly coloured cocktails as if they are life belts thrown into the raging sea.

Three more cocktails later and the atmosphere returns to an easy camaraderie. The earlier tension drowned beneath copious amounts of alcohol.

I'm surprised when Catherine nudges me and whispers, "That man over there can't take his eyes off you."

"What man?"

I turn around, and she hisses, "Don't look. He'll know we're talking about him."

I stare at her in confusion, and she giggles, "Why don't we wander over to the edge and I'll take your photograph. You can get a peek at him from there and see if I'm imagining it or not."

"Okay." I sense my eyes light up because I've always enjoyed soliciting male attention and Catherine says loudly, "We're just going to grab a photo. We won't be long."

Then Sonia ruins it as always and yells, "A photo! What a great idea. We'll all go and take one as a memento of my birthday."

I roll my eyes as Samantha catches my expression and she giggles behind her hand because ever since we were at school, Sonia has always had the skill of making just about everything about her.

We stand and move to the edge of the terrace and as we line up, Sonia shouts across to the waiter, "Can you take a photo for us, please?"

The fact he's serving another table is a little awkward, and then my heart flutters when a deep voice says, "I will."

Catherine nudges me as the man rises from his table and walks toward us, his gaze lingering on mine, and I see what all the fuss is about. If anything, my breath pauses because this man is gorgeous. He has the dark swarthy good looks of a native and is dressed immaculately in black tailored trousers with a crisp white shirt open to reveal a broad masculine chest. His dark hair is neatly styled and his sexy brown eyes glitter as they stare at me long and hard.

It resembles a scene from a Mills and Boon novel and just like the fluttering heroines, I'm equally affected and as he draws near, Sonia says loudly, "Great, thanks."

She thrusts her phone into his hand and gathers us around her like a mother hen and it takes all my concentration not to stare with my mouth open at an example of the most romantic hero I have ever met.

Several photos later, we thank the gentleman and return to our table and Catherine whispers, "What do you think?"

"I'm in love." I giggle, my earlier dour mood evaporating like droplets of rain in this desert.

"It's a shame he just left."

My heart sinks as I nod. "It is."

"Mind you, if you did live here, I'm guessing you would have your pick of men like that." She reassures me with a smile and suddenly, just like that, the move to Dubai is sealed.

―――

Throughout dinner, I can't get the stranger out of my mind, and I imagine all kinds of scenarios where he declares his undying love for me and whisks me away to a penthouse in the city, lavishing me with limitless credit cards. This is definitely the land of opportunity, and I am determined to make it home, so I chat to Samantha through dinner about how we can make that happen.

By the time the evening ends, I'm so fired up, I am inclined to grab my laptop and start the ball rolling but perhaps it's the jet lag, or the number of cocktails I've consumed but I suddenly feel exceptionally tired and decide to head back to my room and call it a night.

My friends obviously have more stamina than me because they decide to order liqueurs and as I make my way to my room, I wonder about the state of their livers.

Surely, it can't be good for them. I mean, I like a drink but not on this scale and I absolutely hate the effect it has on me the next day.

By the time the lift reaches me, I'm dead on my feet and as I lean against the mirrored walls, I hope I'm able to make it to my room before I collapse with exhaustion.

Just as the doors are about to shut, somebody rushes in and my heart flutters when I recognise the man from earlier.

The doors close, leaving me inside with the man of my dreams and he smiles in recognition as I gaze at him in drunken awe.

"We meet again." He says with a wicked smile, and I sense myself blushing as I say shyly, "Um, thanks for taking the photograph earlier."

"You are welcome." He leans against the wall and the burning look he directs my way could melt the polar ice caps, causing me to shift awkwardly on my feet.

"Tell me about your situation." He says suddenly and I stare at him in confusion.

"What situation?"

"Your friends. What is the occasion?"

"Oh." I grin. "We're celebrating my friend's birthday with a few days away."

"I see."

He stares a little harder. "What does your husband think about his wife going off without him?"

"I wouldn't know. I don't have a husband."

The way his eyes light up causes my breath to hitch because we are definitely having a moment here and I'm not sure if it's my imagination or not, but he shifts a little closer and whispers, "That's good to hear."

"Why?"

My heart is beating so fast I swear he can hear it and I'm shocked when he reaches out and tucks my hair behind my ear and says huskily, "I would like to get to know you better. Maybe over breakfast."

"Um…" I am lost for words as he stares at me waiting for an answer and I nod, my eyes glazing over at the intoxicating scent of his aftershave and dominant personality that is stifling me right now.

"Is that yes?" He strokes my face and I swear I couldn't move now if I tried and I nod, the lump in my throat a barrier to my words.

The lift stops at my floor, but I make no move to leave because, as it turns out, I don't want to go anywhere.

The door closes and we travel up and he smiles softly, "You missed your stop."

"Did I?" I don't know where this woman is coming from, but I like her because suddenly everything I want in life is in this lift.

His lips crash against mine at lightning speed and we become a mass of tangled limbs and hot fervent kisses as he presses me against the mirrored walls. It's intoxicating, forbidden and foolish, and I am so blaming the alcohol in the morning.

Right now, it's good to be me because the only one I'm betraying is myself and my shattered principles and as we spill out into the hallway, he tugs me at speed to his room and I don't look back.

8

GINNY

There's a slight crack in the curtains, letting the light in as if heaven beckons and from the state of my head and body, I danced with the devil last night.

The heat caressing my skin is tempting, but the man lying beside me is even more. I should be embarrassed, devastated even, but how can I be when I just enjoyed the night of my life?

His name is Omar, and that is all I know, because talking wasn't a high priority last night.

He stares at me through those devilish eyes with wicked intent and once again, my heart flutters and my dark soul rejoices as he leans in to kiss my greedy lips.

I drown in decadence as I do something forbidden and slightly out of character, but not unusual for me. I've never been one to shy away from male attention and, being an independent woman, I've never had to consider anyone's opinions or feelings other than my own.

"Spend the day with me." He says huskily, as he strokes my face lightly and I shiver with pleasure because he gives me nothing else.

"My friends." I whisper, and his eyes flash with mischief.

"What would they think if they saw you now?"

"A mixture of jealously and disapproval, I'm guessing."

I grin as he smiles seductively, and my heart is torn between wanting more of him or heading to breakfast to meet up with my friends as arranged to gloat about my good fortune.

"They won't miss you. Call your friend and say you're sick."

He is very persuasive, and I wrestle with my demons as I fight to do what I want over what I should.

"What about you, Omar? Don't you have business to attend to?" I say slightly breathlessly as his hand dips lower, causing a startled gasp to spill from my lips.

"Only the business of you."

He laughs and rolls onto his back, dragging my head to his insanely ripped chest.

"My business concluded yesterday."

His deep voice is comforting as he divulges a little information about himself.

"I'm in Dubai for business. Tomorrow, I move to Saudi and then onto London."

"What do you do?" I'm curious and he smiles.

"Investments mainly. I own a private company and look after the interests of several powerful clients. I'm in demand because wealth is taken extremely seriously here, and I'm on call twenty-four seven to take care of their assets."

"You're coming to London. Where are you staying?"

"I have an apartment not far from the river."

He kisses the top of my head. "I hope you will visit me there."

I glance up and note the intensity in his eyes as his request hangs in the air and I whisper, "You want to see me again?"

"Of course." He shakes his head. "Don't you?"

"Of course, but I thought..."

"What did you think, my love?"

My heart flutters like a schoolgirl and I say with a deep breath, "I suppose I thought this was one night only. A moment of madness and I would never see you again."

"Then you have a low opinion of yourself, because why would I want that?"

He pulls my face to his and whispers, "I travel a lot. I'm never home. I have apartments in most cities of the world and the only reason I'm here is because I sold my apartment in Dubai and my new one isn't ready yet. Our paths have crossed inexplicably, and I believe for a reason, and I will not ignore what could be the beginning of something good."

I am delirious with lust and desire and blinded to common sense. Every word he speaks is like a gift to my ego. There is a small part of me that is lapping this attention up and another larger part of me that's waving a host of red flags and telling me to grow up and be an adult for once.

I ignore those flags but keep them in mind and smile, whispering, "I agree. I have no ties and no man in my life, so why not?"

He nods and I don't miss the triumphant gleam in his eye

and yet once again my vanity tells me it's because he's got what he wants – me.

Then it occurs to me to ask him more about his life and I say with interest, "What about you? Are you single because I find that incredibly hard to believe?"

He laughs out loud and pulls me even tighter against him.

"I never married. My life is not suited to a family one. I've had many women; I will not apologise for that, but I never cheat, and I never promise anything I can't deliver."

"I see."

I'm not sure where this leaves me, and he grips my face and stares deep into my eyes and says with a husky drawl. "Right now, you are *my* woman, Ginny. You are in my arms and in my bed. I am not looking for another and I am desperate to hold on to you, so as a businessman, let me lay a proposal on the table."

I swear my heart turns inside out at his choice of words because what the hell is happening in my life right now?

"Let's get to know one another, enjoy each other's company, and meet up when I'm in London. You can travel on business with me if you want to and we can see where this attraction leads us."

"So soon." I stare at him in shock because this one night stand is turning out to be something else entirely.

"Why wait?" He shrugs.

"We are not kids and don't have time to waste with courtship and dates. We are old enough to know the risks involved, but young enough to ignore them. What do you say? Take a chance and see where this leads, or walk away with a nice memory when you are back in your cold country?"

He makes a good argument and I grin. Any doubts I have trampled at my feet in my rush to take him up on his offer.

"I would love to see where this goes, Omar."

As we seal the deal in a far less conventional way, I can't believe my luck. This is like a story from the most intense romance novel, and I'm almost assured of a happily ever after with my rich Arab lover.

9
GINNY

I float down to breakfast on a cloud of euphoria. I swear every inch of me is glowing as I enjoyed the night of my life.

I am the last one to arrive and several pairs of eyes stare at me in surprise as I sink into my seat and groan. "I need a cup of tea, and fast."

"What happened to you?" Samantha says with surprise and from the curious faces staring back at me, I'm wearing my shame for all to see.

"You are never going to believe what happened after I left you last night." I say with a smug expression.

"Something happened, are you ok?" Amanda says quickly

and I grin broadly. "Do you remember the stranger who took our photograph?"

Sammy nods. "I remember him."

I peer at Catherine, who appears worried.

"We shared a lift to our rooms and, as it turned out, only one of them was occupied last night."

"Oh my God, Ginny, you didn't." Catherine gasps and I nod, sipping my tea like the cat who got the cream.

"It was fun. A wild experience that I seized with both hands and why not? I'm single."

"But he could have been a rapist, or a murderer, a criminal even." Sonia gasps and from the disapproving expressions on my friend's faces, jealously has yet to reveal itself. I should be ashamed of myself judging by their expressions, but I'm not, and I say with a giggle, "He wants to see me again. In fact, he wants me to spend the day with him before he heads to Saudi later today."

"Ginny." Sonia says in her best matron voice. "I strongly urge you to step back and approach this with common sense. This man could be anyone, and if you go off with him, we may never see you again."

"Don't be so melodramatic." I say as I scrape back my chair and sigh. "I'm a grown woman and can make my own choices and right now I need food and fast."

I leave them to talk about me behind my back and head to the glorious buffet that is stretched out before me like a king's banquet. I wish I had never told them now because, far from being envious, they are glaring at me as if I'm a fool and nobody likes to feel like that.

I tell myself they don't know the situation and I suppose looking in on it, it's pretty crazy, but I can't ignore the happiness being with Omar has given me and if it goes nowhere, at least I can hold on to the experience. I'm not a fool. I know it probably won't last, but until that happens, I'm taking full advantage of the fairy story that is unfolding in my life.

After breakfast, I head to my room to change because Omar is taking me on a city tour to show me the sights. I told my friends I would be back just after lunch and then they would have my full attention because later today Omar is heading to Saudi on business.

I pull on a maxi dress that covers my arms and hangs low to the ground and I grab my bag containing my sunglasses and purse.

As I wait on the balcony, it's hitting home a bit. I slept with a stranger. A man I never met before and allowed him to do unspeakable things to my body. I'm a slut. A mad sex crazed harlot and I should be ashamed of myself. My friends certainly are, and yet I am jumping into the fire and will have to live with the burns.

A gentle knock on the door brings me back to reality and my heart flutters when I see Omar standing there, looking every bit as delicious as he did last night.

"You look beautiful, Ginny." His lazy gaze drags over my body, leaving it bristling with the need for his attention.

"Same for you, Omar."

I'm not even kidding because he does, irresistible in fact. He is wearing a smart pair of black trousers and a black silk shirt, open just enough to reveal the toned abs of a man who looks after himself. His leather belt is snaked around his hips, and I can tell it's expensive and the gold Rolex on his wrist could be distasteful to some but oozes wealth and charisma just like the man wearing it.

"Are you ready, my love?"

He extends his hand and mine slips into his as if it was born to. Then I follow him to the lift to begin the first day of the rest of my life.

———

We make our way outside, and the waiting valet tosses Omar a set of keys and moves to hold the door open for me. I blink in astonishment at the black Ferrari that is waiting for us, with brown leather seats and opulence that is like a drug to me.

Omar jumps into the driver's seat, and I stare at him in awe because I must be asleep and am starring in my perfect fantasy.

He removes a pair of black shades from the glove compartment and says in a deep voice.

"Let me show you Dubai."

I am speechless as we pull away from the luxury hotel and head off on the road adjacent to the man-made palm where we are staying.

As I gaze out of the window, I stare at a place that has been carefully contrived. Built in the desert to appeal to the greed in everyone. The fact I'm greedier than most makes this my land of opportunity because my move here is assured after the last twenty-four hours.

Omar points out various landmarks that I have seen on Instagram posts and in the news and a shiver of excitement passes through me as I salivate over the vista before me.

It's almost too much and as he pulls into the lobby of the newest five-star hotel, he says casually, "Come, the view from the restaurant at the top is breath-taking."

"Are we allowed to go inside?" I'm in awe of my surroundings and he nods, a small smile of affection gracing his lips.

"Of course, it's a business and they rely on profits. We can take coffee here and decide where to go next."

I thought our hotel was amazing, but this one has torn up the blueprint because all around me are marble floors, polished mirrors and sculptures that would look more at home in an art gallery. It's as if I've stepped into another world and I stare at the glass pyramid that is made from multiple pieces of coloured glass that tower in the centre of the amazing lobby.

Omar leads me to a golden lift and slips his hand in mine as we wait for it to come and leans down and whispers, "I want to spoil you, my love. You deserve it."

I really think I do because up until now, nobody has ever really tried.

I always wanted passion in my life. To be the centre of someone's world and adored even. The best I've had so far is dinner, followed by sex, courtesy of the men I met on my dating app. There was one man who had potential, but he turned out to be married all the time. However, nobody has ever made me feel so special and if it all fizzles away like the bubbles from the champagne that's in abundance here, I couldn't care less because I'm here now and experiencing something so amazing, it has made my entire life.

Omar wasn't wrong, the view is outstanding and as a waiter directs us to a table overlooking the view, I allow the gentle breeze to caress my heated skin as we sit at a table that was designed for intimacy.

The white tablecloth is rigid and crease free on which an exotic flower rests beside a flickering candle which is simple and chic.

Omar leans back in his seat and peruses the menu that the waiter left and then glances up and his eyes glitter as he says firmly, "I will order for both of us."

"Ok."

I lean on my elbows and gaze at him dreamily as he orders speciality coffees and a selection of pastries.

He snaps the menu shut and as soon as the waiter leaves, he leans forward and takes my hands in his.

"Thank you."

"What for?" I sense myself blushing as his dark, sensuous eyes pierce my soul.

"For agreeing to this. To me."

My heart almost stops beating as he kisses my hands and gazes into my eyes the entire time, and I swear I have never felt anything remotely like the emotions he pulls from inside me.

"I will be in London in five days time. Give me your contact details and I will arrange everything."

"Everything?" I'm puzzled, and he kisses my fingers one by one and then says in a deliciously sexy voice, "I don't want to waste a second of my time there with you. I will be in London for one week before I head to New York. We will take that time to test our compatibility and if we still feel the same, we can move forward."

"Really?" My heart is thumping because this is a little intense and quite overwhelming really and he nods, a slow grin spreading across his handsome face that makes me smile.

"I don't want to waste time like a lovesick teenager. We are past all of that. I'm successful because I see an opportunity and I act on it. This is no different, so why take things slow when we are both of the same mind?"

"It's just, well, things like this don't happen to me and it's a little overwhelming, if I'm honest."

Omar nods and I love how his dark eyes glitter as he whispers, "Then the men you have met are fools. Trust me,

Ginny, a woman like you is a treasure for any man and I will not let this opportunity pass me by. You can be assured that I treat my women like queens, and you will never want for anything. Allow me to look after you. That's all I ask and all I desire is your company and loyalty in return."

The waiter stops by with the order, but Omar doesn't drop my hand for a second, and it's almost as if the waiter isn't here, which is a little embarrassing really as he sets the order down around us.

Then, as he leaves, Omar whispers, "Now we eat and then we continue our journey – together."

Dubai is certainly hot, and I never really believed it could get hotter, but suddenly I'm on fire and incapable of making my own decisions. I already know I am intoxicated by this man and if even half of what he promises comes true, I will be the happiest woman alive.

10

SONIA

I can't believe what Ginny has done. I organised this trip so we could all spend quality time together and she has made it all about her.

When she left, the others were as disgusted as I am and as I prepare myself for a day by the pool, I hope she regrets her decision.

Amanda is in her room and it's good to enjoy some time alone. It was good of her to book the trip, but I would have preferred a suite of my own, really. Even though she's my best friend, she can be a little irritating at times, and I can never switch off when she's around.

I lean on the balcony and study the view, loving how

bright and clean everywhere is. It's certainly different to my view of home, causing my thoughts to turn to Daniel and I wonder what he is doing now — or whom?

I sigh when I picture my husband who I met at my eighteenth birthday party. He was a friend of my current boyfriend who I ditched as soon as Daniel showed me any attention. I was infatuated with him, certainly at the beginning, and when he left college and started working in Canary Wharf, I thought our future was guaranteed.

I'm not sure when fate decided to play with me, but it never really turned out to be the amazing dream I hoped it would be.

Daniel, as it turned out, isn't that great at his job and despite securing many amazing positions and earning shed loads of money at the beginning, he never really held onto it. I've lost count of how many positions he's taken and I'm always worried that our dream life will end on the edge of one of his bad errors of judgement.

Then there's Jasper and Amanda, living the life I always wanted as mine; the life I deserve and if I knew then what I know now, I would never have introduced them and kept Jasper for myself.

"Sonia."

My heart sinks when Amanda calls from my open doorway.

"Are you ready?"

With a sigh, I head back inside and plaster a smile on my face.

"Yes, I'll just grab my bag."

I lift it from the beautiful blue and gold embroidered chair and look with envy at my friend. Her long blonde hair is tied back in a scrunchie, and her oversized designer sunglasses make her face appear small and petite.

The sarong she is wearing probably costs several hundreds of pounds and her rings sparkle as they capture the sunlight.

Amanda is a poster girl for women who have it all and I try so hard to keep up with her. She always has a permanent suntan and has no worries or insecurities. She is a woman who has everything that should have been mine.

"It's going to be a hot one." She says conversationally, and I nod. "I can't wait. It's so good to ditch February and flee to the scorching desert."

She laughs. "It was a good idea."

"That you made happen." I remind her and she nods. "I always do."

If I detect a slight edge to her voice, I ignore it because Amanda needs to realise that she has everything because of me. Her husband, her fine living and her friends. She was never a Summerhouse girl, just an honorary member because of me, and she should be grateful for that. I have given her friends, something she could never manage on her own, and because we were thrown together as children, she was accepted as one of us.

The others like her. It's obvious and over the years the lines have blurred, and our beginnings have been forgotten. She's one of us now, at least she should be, but I realise it's always in the back of her mind that she's here by invitation only.

"Shall we take our usual beds by the lifeguard?" She says as we step out into the sunshine and regard the almost empty pool area."

"Guys, over here." A loud voice greets us, and I stare irritably at Samantha as she waves from a position in the opposite direction. Catherine is next to her and they have two free beds beside them, causing me to groan.

"That will never do. Don't they realise those beds will be in the shade after lunch?"

"I guess not." Amanda says softly beside me, and I point to the ones near the lifeguard and yell, "These are better. Trust me."

I don't even hang around and head to my preferred option, expecting the others to gather their stuff and join us.

Amanda hesitates and I say with a sigh, "They'll thank me later."

The pool man jumps up as we approach and unrolls the towels that are placed on each of the bed and smiles. "I will bring you an ice bucket with water. Please call me if you would like to order any drinks."

"Thanks." I nod as I settle on my bed, reaching for my sunscreen and making sure my face is shaded by the giant umbrella.

Amanda does the same and we watch the others carrying their stuff over to join us.

"Those beds will be in the shade after lunch." I say as they draw near. "We would have to move, and these beds may not be available."

"Oh, thanks." Samantha says, taking the vacant bed next to mine, and Catherine takes the one beside Amanda.

"This place is amazing. I never expected it to be so, well, posh actually." Samantha says with a sigh, and I feel a little smug as I nod my agreement. "Only the best for the Summerhouse girls." I say with a smile, and Samantha laughs. "It seems that way."

Catherine sprays her body with sunscreen and says with interest, "I wonder what Ginny's doing now. That man was seriously attractive."

Amanda nods. "He was. It's like something out of a movie."

"Let's hope it is not a horror one then." I snap, causing Catherine to giggle nervously.

"What if it's genuine, and he is the most amazing catch?" Samantha says dreamily, and I bark out a laugh. "It's just a fantasy, mark my words. I mean, ask yourself why he's still single if he's so amazing."

"I guess." Samantha says, with a hint of disappointment.

"She's a fool." I say with a shrug. "We should watch her; he could be a criminal and is using her as a drugs mule or something."

"Do you really think that?" Catherine says in horror, and I nod.

"Why not? You see it on the news all the time. Handsome man flatters a gullible woman and the next thing you know she's taking stuff into the country for him. I'm just glad we're in business class and won't need to be associated with her. The rest of you should walk apart from her through customs, just in case."

"Sonia!" Amanda says in shock, causing me to laugh. "What? I'm only stating the facts. Have a go at me when she lives happily ever after, but until then I'm reserving judgement."

I lean back and pull on my sunglasses and close my eyes, effectively shutting them all out.

I definitely had too much to drink last night, and my head is still pounding. Come to think of it, I *always* have too much to drink, and I can't ignore the fact anymore that it's becoming a problem in every sense of the word.

I'm not sure when I first noticed I was out of control. I suppose it was after I discovered Daniel's second affair. He promised me that the first one was a one off, a mistake, and so I forgave him. But the second one was with a mum from the school, who he met when he took over the school run while I was having James.

Daniel was on paternity leave and struck up a friendship with Lucinda Wilson. The affair was short-lived, but the recriminations lasted the rest of the time the boys were at that school. It's only when we moved away and sent our boys to private school that we got shot of the stares and knowing glances from the playground mums.

I shiver as I remember what a difficult time that was. At least in private school, the mums were a little more refined. Daniel was never allowed on the school run again, but that didn't stop the affairs.

For some reason, the tears well up behind my sunglasses as I struggle to deal with the problems that man has caused in my outwardly respectable life and the fact that one of his indiscretions is on this same trip doesn't make it feel any better. No, marriage to Daniel was my biggest mistake and I'm the fool who chose to live with it.

11

SONIA

The day is spent sunbathing and drinking, which is the best way to pass the time in my opinion, and it's even better when Samantha informs us that it's raining at home.

"When isn't it?" I grumble and Amanda sighs.

"We're lucky we can take some time away from it. Not everybody is that lucky."

"You make your own luck in life." I say irritably and Catherine adds, "To a degree, but not everybody has that luxury. I mean, what if you're struggling and can't get a job? You may be ill and unable to work. There are a million reasons why not everyone can do well for themselves through no fault of their own."

"If you say so." I gather my things and shake my head.

"I see Ginny never made it back. Should we inform the authorities?"

"Really?" Samantha says aghast, and Catherine laughs. "Call off the search party. Look what the cat dragged in."

I peer over to where she's pointing and watch Ginny heading towards us with a huge grin on her face and a designer shopping bag in her hand.

I stare at her in surprise because she looks different somehow. Happy for once which transforms her usual surly features into a countenance of joy. If anything, she's shed a few years too and whatever this guy is feeding her must be priceless.

She reaches us and sits on the edge of Amanda's sun-bed and giggles.

"Ladies. Did you miss me?"

"I want to hear every last delicious piece of information." Samantha says with excitement, and we all sit and watch the transformation of our friend happening before our eyes.

I stare at her in shock as she lifts the bag and says smugly, "Look what Omar bought me."

"Is that ...?" Catherine whispers with hushed reverence.

"Chanel. Yes, it is."

"Is it genuine?" I say with a roll of my eyes and Ginny grins. "If the Chanel shop in the Dubai Mall is in the habit of peddling fakes, then you may be right. However, I doubt it because I saw the price tag."

"They don't come cheap." Samantha says with envy.

"You're right. There's no way I could afford one at home, let alone here where everything is more expensive." Ginny says with a smug smile.

"You are so lucky?' Samantha shakes her head in astonishment and Amanda reaches out, "May I?"

"Of course." Ginny hands her the bag and Amanda explores every inch of it with a smile.

"It's gorgeous. If I'm not mistaken, it's from this season's collection. You are lucky not to have to go on a waiting list."

"Omar knew the right things to say because the shop assistant told us it was reserved and then five minutes later, she was wrapping it up. He certainly knows how to get what he wants."

"You could say that." I reply, ignoring the warning glare Amanda throws at me.

"What's the matter Sonia, are you jealous?" Ginny teases, but she will never realise how accurate her question is. Pushing my jealously aside, I plaster a smile on my face and try to look happy for her.

"A little if I'm honest. I mean, nobody has ever treated me as well as he has treated you already and you've known him for less than twenty-four hours. Can you imagine what will happen after a month, or a few years down the line?"

"If we make it that far."

I stare at her in surprise as she exhales sharply.

"What do you think, girls? Is this too good to be true?"

"Possibly, but strange things do happen, and it may be fate." Amanda says kindly, and Ginny glances at her with a hopeful smile.

"I suppose. It's just that it all seems too good to be true. *He* is definitely too good to be true and I'm kind of pinching myself a bit."

"What happened today?" Catherine interrupts and Ginny's eyes soften as she remembers the past few hours.

"Well, first we had a snack at that new hotel on the rooftop terrace."

"Lucky you." Samantha sighs and I'm inclined to agree with her.

"Then we went on a city tour where Omar pointed out the various landscapes and buildings, telling me a little about them and their history."

She leans back and tucks her feet under her as she basks in the last remaining rays of the sun and says dreamily. "He took me for lunch at a restaurant in the marina. Lobster and caviar which was the best thing I have ever tasted."

"You're making me hungry." Catherine grumbles, reminding us we should really head back inside and change for dinner.

"After lunch, we drove to the Dubai Mall for a spot of shopping. I was a little intimidated by it if I'm honest. I mean, the shops were way out of my league, but Omar insisted on visiting every one."

"Wow, it's like something out of Pretty Woman." Samantha says with excitement, and Ginny nods.

"It certainly felt like that. Anyway, we ended up in Chanel and I don't know about you, Amanda aside, but I never dreamed I'd own one myself. Omar asked me which one I liked, and I pointed this one out. I really thought we were only window shopping, and I was amazed and completely embarrassed when he insisted on buying it for me. I tried to talk him out of it, but he has a habit of being so, well, persuasive and I doubt anything can change his mind once it's made up."

She lifts the bag and hugs it close to her chest and laughs happily. "He told me it's a parting gift. Something special to remember our first date by and he hopes there will be many more to come."

"Well, I must hand it to you, Ginny. I'm impressed."

Catherine says with admiration. "You certainly hit the jackpot with him."

"I know."

Ginny is positively beaming, and I don't believe I have ever seen her looking so happy in all the years I've known her.

"So, what happens now?" I say practically, and she grins. "He left for Saudi on business, and I've promised to meet him in London in five days' time."

"He's coming to England?" Samantha says in awe, and Ginny nods enthusiastically. "He has an apartment by the river and asked me to meet him. He travels a lot and tells me I could even go with him if I had the time."

I stare at her thoughtfully. "Did he ask you to take anything back for him?"

"Sonia!" Amanda interrupts quickly, and I shrug.

"I'm only asking. It all seems too good to be true if you ask me."

"I thought that too," Ginny admits, looking a little doubtful. "I mean, I'm not an idiot. I realise this is unusual and he could have an ulterior motive. I'm not a young impressionable girl, just an old impressionable woman." She laughs out loud. "And do you know what? I don't care if he is playing me for a fool. The only thing he's given me is this Chanel bag and the only other person who touched it was the store assistant. If he did plant anything in it, he must be a magician."

I nod with a smile. "Then I take it all back. In fact..." I stare at her with an envious smile and say with a sigh, "I wish I was you."

She says incredulously. "You do?"

I nod, a little of my burden shifting as I say sadly, "I probably shouldn't say anything, but well, Daniel and I are having problems and this trip couldn't have come at a better time for me."

Now I have their full attention and Amanda reaches out and strokes my arm in a compassionate move.

"Do you want to talk about it?"

I sense every pair of eyes boring into me as I shake my head and force a lightness into my tone that I am definitely not feeling.

"It's fine. We'll be ok. Perhaps we've reached that time when couples are so familiar with one another, the magic evaporated. I'm sure we'll be fine. I mean, this trip may make Daniel realise what it's like when I'm not around. He'll probably beg me never to leave him again after a few days with Thomas and James."

I stand and gather my bag and say loudly, "Anyway, we need cocktails and to hear more about Ginny's exciting adventure, not my troubles. This is a party, after all, and we must make the most of our freedom while we have it."

I walk away because the thought of alcohol is very attractive right now and as I catch Samantha's eye, she looks away, reminding me that if anyone knows what Daniel's like, it's her.

12

AMANDA

I'm already weary and wish I'd never agreed to this. I find it difficult to act normally when inside my rage is threatening to boil over.

I'm not sure when my friendship with Sonia changed. I can't even put a finger on it. It's a cancer that started small and grew before I realised it was there. I've left it too long and now it's inoperable and threatens my life, or at least life as I know it.

If I feel regret, it's that I did it in the first place and yet how could I not?

I owed her. If it wasn't for Sonia, my life would be very

different, and I would never have met Jasper. I wouldn't have my adored children and I wouldn't be here now.

The trouble is, when is a debt truly settled? It's as if I've been paying her back for years and I suppose inevitably it will come to a head one day.

Jasper told me to let it go. It wasn't worth the irritation, but I disagree. It's worth driving the point home because I feel used and that's not a nice feeling to have.

"Amanda!" she calls me from the small room that joins ours and with a sigh, I spray on some cologne and head off to find her.

"Is this dress ok?"

She pirouettes on the spot, and I smile like the dutiful friend I am.

"Amazing. Is it new?"

"Yes. Don't tell Daniel, but I treated myself for my birthday. He can't argue with that because it's not every day a woman turns fifty."

She laughs and I try to shake the despondency inside me that's growing by the minute and say with a smile. "We should head off and find the others. It is happy hour, after all, and we don't want to waste that opportunity."

"Definitely not." Sonia pulls her pashmina around her bare shoulders and grabs her bag.

"Come on then. I can't wait to hear about Ginny's day in more detail. I still can't believe she did that."

"It's quite romantic when you think about it."

"Really?" Sonia laughs out loud.

"I would describe it as foolish, reckless and a bad decision. I mean, we're not getting any younger and sleeping with a stranger is the stuff of madness. He could be riddled with disease or have secretly filmed it for the internet. She should be more careful."

"Why?" I shrug and Sonia peers at me in surprise.

"She's single, has no children, and a very good job. If anything, I admire her because she knows what she wants and doesn't care what other people think. I applaud her and wish I was like her."

"You are," Sonia says incredulously. "I mean, you have it all, Amanda. If there is one person among us who deserves that title, it's you."

"I guess." I feel bad because Sonia's right. I am lucky, but I don't think about my life in that way. It's normal to me and most of my time is spent being a wife and a mother and I don't have time to congratulate myself on winning the marriage lottery. We still have our problems like most couples do and my job title is still the same as it's always been. I've never had a career of my own because I met Jasper fresh from college and we married in a whirlwind, and I never needed to work.

"Sometimes I wonder what life would be like if I hadn't met Jasper."

"Are you mad?" Sonia raises her eyes.

"Imagine if you had to work like the rest of us. You wouldn't find life so easy then."

Sonia worked at a bank when she left school for at least a year before she married Daniel, so she speaks from experience, but I don't believe either of us has the right to comment on working women. We never were.

We head downstairs to the bar where Catherine is already waiting, chatting with the waiter.

She smiles as we approach and says with excitement, "I've ordered us all the house cocktail."

"Which is?"

Sonia slides into the seat opposite and Catherine giggles. "Porn star martinis."

We share a grin and, as the waiter heads off, Catherine lowers her voice. "I wasn't sure they would offer cocktails. I always thought Dubai frowned on drinking of any kind."

"They do but realise this is a business and they need to relax the rules to encourage tourists here." Sonia says as if she knows everything as always, and Catherine nods.

"I suppose, but I still don't know what I can and can't do."

I stifle a smile as I note her dress covering her entire body, right to her neck.

Catherine has never been one to step out of line and is horrified if the rules are even bent, let alone broken. It's why I was surprised when her husband invested in Daniel's property portfolio. Knowing his track record, it wasn't the safest of investments which proved right when the market crashed last year, and they lost everything. It was a terrible time, and I wondered if their friendship would survive but as always, Sonia turned the whole fiasco around to make her and Daniel the victims and Catherine and Connor retreated to lick their wounds and work even harder to inflate their dwindling bank account.

The others soon join us, and I'm amused to see Ginny clutching the Chanel bag as if it's a gold bar and I suppose, given the price, it is.

"You could have left your bag in the room. We aren't going anywhere," Sonia says, sounding a little disgruntled, and Ginny shakes her head. "This bag is not leaving my sight even for a second. I've never had anything so valuable, and it won't fit in the safe."

We burst out laughing at the image of Ginny trying to stuff the designer bag into the hotel room safe and she grasps one of the cocktails that the waiter is handing out and grins.

"Allow me to toast the occasion."

We stare at her expectantly, and she grins. "To turning

fifty and realising every dream we ever had. To new beginnings and chapters yet to be scripted. To our past and our future and to our families and friends who can't be with us."

I suppress a giggle as Sonia throws me an amused glance as Ginny holds up her bag and says with a smirk. "And to many more of these and more of the same with my new man."

We raise our glasses and drain them at record speed and, as Sonia hails the waiter, I settle in for a long night ahead.

13
AMANDA

After dinner, we decide to take advantage of the free shuttle service to the Dubai Mall that is open until midnight. Apparently, there's a fountain show that can't be missed, reflected on the side of the Burj Khalifa.

It takes at least forty minutes to get there, and I spend most of the journey staring out of the darkened windows as we take a tour of the city, the high-rise blocks appearing almost new, telling me this place is in constant development.

"Connor would love it here." Catherine says beside me, and I say with interest. "Has he ever been?"

"No." Catherine shrugs. "I don't know why. I suppose it's

because he's so busy at home he never has time to go away unless it benefits business in some way."

"But you take holidays." I'm surprised, and she nods.

"Yes, we do, but only once a year and for two weeks only. He won't allow us any more time than that."

Catherine falls silent and I wonder about her life. She never seems happy really, and there was a time when I thought she was going to leave Connor. I hoped she would because I've never liked him. Overbearing and pompous, with an inflated ego that doesn't go unnoticed. I always thought Catherine was embarrassed by him. The odd times our husbands were involved in meeting up, he always tried to dominate Jasper's time and talk business. So much it became a problem, causing to Jasper to shy away from any events where Connor would be.

We have turned down endless invitations to dinner and even the odd trip away because Jasper can't stand the man, which places me in a difficult position with my friend, who is the sweetest person I've ever known.

We reach the mall, and it certainly lives up to its reputation as being one of the largest ones in the world.

As we walk through the doors, we are wide eyed and Sonia says in awe, "Okay, here's the plan. If we lose one another, we'll meet at the Apple store in one hour's time. We can watch the fountain show from that entrance, and it will be a good meeting point."

The others nod and accept everything Sonia tells them because old habits die hard, and Sonia has organised our lives for most of them.

My heart sinks when Sonia slips her arm in mine and whispers, "Let's head to the designer area. We can't allow Ginny to have all the fun."

I plaster a smile on my face, but inside my rage is boiling because I know exactly what's coming.

As the other three head off to Bath and Body Works, Sonia drags me in the direction of the more unaffordable shops and it's as if the air changes and becomes more exclusive as we surround ourselves with names that appear in Vogue and on every celebrity wish list I've ever seen. Gucci, Dior and Chanel mix with Burberry, Hermes, and Versace. I've never been bothered by labels before, and Jasper doesn't help when he heads inside the first one he sees at Christmas and my birthday and orders a selection of gifts that he believes I'll love.

I glance down at the rings on my fingers and my Cartier watch that was a present on our last anniversary. He means well, but I would much rather have more of his time than the brightly coloured boxes that arrive courtesy of Royal Mail.

We are strangers who live together. Both of us settling into roles that have sort of moulded around us. I am brought out on the odd occasion plus ones are involved and even on weekends he prefers to spend most of his time in his study, catching up with correspondence and checking on his private investments.

It's as if I am a single mum whose main occupation was raising our three children and ferrying them to clubs and football matches. It was riding for the girls and rugby for Freddie, and I envied my friends whose husbands took their turn on the weekend. Jasper never does. I should be grateful, and I am, but watching Ginny receive deserved attention from her romantic stranger has highlighted a yearning I've kept buried for quite some time now.

My husband's attention.

Sonia distracts me from my thoughts by pulling me into

several shops and soon narrows down her choice to a pair of Jimmy Choo's or a Hermes scarf. Both have eye watering price tags, and she wrinkles up her nose and says with genuine confusion. "I can't choose between them."

"Get both then." I say uninterested, wishing we could meet the others and grab a coffee before the fountain show.

"Well, I suppose it is my birthday. I do deserve a treat."

She smiles broadly. "Thanks bestie, you're such a great friend."

We head to the checkout, and she hands the shoes over to the assistant and whispers, "We'll grab these before heading back to Hermes."

As the assistant rings up the purchase, she smiles pleasantly and tells us the amount owed, and Sonia rummages in her bag and huffs. "Great, I left my purse back at the hotel. I'm so forgetful sometimes." She sighs and turns to me with an apologetic smile. "I don't suppose you…"

"Of course." I present my own credit card and Sonia hugs me, whispering, "You're such a good friend. I don't know what I'd do without you."

As the assistant deals with the transaction, I smile and pretend that I'm ok with this, but all it does is remind me what a gullible fool I am.

As we head outside, I make to go in the direction of the Apple shop and Sonia pulls me back and says with a small whisper, "Let's go and pick up the scarf too. I'll settle up with you later."

She doesn't even wait for my response and just pulls me along after her and doesn't stop until she is holding the scarf in her hands.

Once again, I give in and pay for the scarf and as we head off to meet the others, my anger is burning away the last shred of our friendship.

I suppose this trip was always going to go one way. It's either make or break for Sonia and me and I'm not certain our friendship will survive another few days, let alone another thirty years.

14

CATHERINE

I feel a little guilty that I bought myself a candle at Bath and Body Works, especially because they are cheaper at home, but it was so tempting when the others were selecting their own favourites and once again, I bowed to peer pressure when they encouraged me to spend some money.

I'm sure it was to make them feel better about their own purchases, and I suppose it could have been worse. I could have been tagging along with Sonia and Amanda, who I'm sure wouldn't be seen dead attacking the sale in Bath and Body Works in favour of Jo Malone or an even more expensive brand.

We make our way to the Apple store and meet up with our friends and as we head outside to the fountains, the warm air hits me and provides a welcome shot of energy.

I love the heat. I always have, and yet Connor isn't a fan because he burns easily and the humidity messes with his complexion.

As usual, when I think about my husband, my heart pounds as if giving up is preferable to a future.

Sammy walks beside me and whispers with concern, "Are you ok, Cathy? You seem quiet."

"I'm fine." I plaster a brilliant smile on my face and hide behind it, as usual. Nobody will ever know the deep despair that exists inside me most of the time which is due to only one thing. Connor.

"I expect the others have been melting their husband's credit cards." Sammy says a little wistfully, and I nod.

"It must be nice."

"It must."

She smiles. "Almost as nice as being all together on this trip. I never really expected it. I'm surprised we haven't done it sooner."

"I suppose." I nod, casting my mind back to the argument it caused back at home. Connor was adamant I couldn't go, throwing every excuse under the sun at me by way of verbal bullets.

'We can't afford it.'

'What about Sally?'

'Why are you so selfish?'

'I never treat myself. Why do you want to go away without me?'

I impressed myself by standing firm and not giving in and, if anything, I can be proud of that at least.

"Was Connor ok with you coming?"

Sammy voices the million-dollar question and I surprise myself by answering with honesty for a change.

"Not really."

She throws me a sympathetic glance. "Do you want to talk about it?"

When I see her earnest, concerned expression and reassuring smile, it strangely causes the tears to well up and, in an unguarded moment, my walls crumble.

Before she can react to that, we hear, "Guys, over here."

Just like that, the moment is gone, and I smile bravely. "It's fine."

I turn to the others and say with false happiness, "Make us all jealous and show us what you bought."

I don't miss the designer bags in Sonia's grip and am a little surprised at the glare Amanda is directing at her before she looks down and then plasters a similar smile on her face that I have perfected over the years. It's almost a pivotal moment as my own walls begin to crumble and I recognise that in someone else and my own journey reaches a fork in the road. Have I been mistaken all these years? Is life in my friend's garden not so rosy after all? I am so wrapped up in my own torment, I never for one moment thought my friends were disguising similar pain and it shouldn't, but it makes me feel a lot better about my own predicament.

Sammy touches my arm and whispers, "We need to talk, and I'm not taking no for an answer. When we get back to the hotel, you and I are having that conversation."

The tone of her voice is fierce and as I stare at her, she winks and the determination in her expression tells me that

Sammy is probably the one friend I need right now and this time I will not hide my reality away.

As we head outside into the square, I love the heat that hits me and warms my soul.

"Wow, this is busy. I never expected it to be so crowded." Ginny says in surprise, and Sonia nods. "It's a popular event. Shall we head to the other side and see if there's a better position to watch the show from."

None of us disagree as always and follow her like the well-trained puppy dogs we are as she leads us around the perimeter of the lake towards the railings on the other side that don't appear as crowded.

We manage to squeeze in and wait for the show to start and Ginny whispers, "Have you seen those bags Sonia is carrying? They don't come cheap. I'm dying to see what's inside."

"Me too." We both stare enviously at the bags grasped tightly in Sonia's hand and Ginny says with a hint of smugness, "I know how that feels now, thanks to Omar."

"Have you heard from him?"

I'm interested because Ginny is living her best life right now, and who wouldn't be interested in that?

"He texted me when we were in Bath and Body Works." From the tone of her voice, it was something she liked, and she purrs with satisfaction. "He told me he was missing me already and would FaceTime me later."

"Things are moving fast then." I'm a little concerned about that, and Ginny nods, her eyes shining with excitement.

"To be honest, Cathy, if I was anyone but me right now, I would consider me a fool. I mean, I met a stranger in the lift and spent the night in his bed. Then I allowed him to buy me an expensive gift and agreed to meet him in London."

She sighs heavily. "I realise this is too good to be true. I'm not dumb enough to believe he has fallen madly in love with me at first sight."

"Really?" I'm shocked because it sounds as if Ginny is upset about that, and she shrugs. "I'm just enjoying it for what it is. If I never see him again and the bag was payment for, well, services rendered, then I'm fine with that."

"You are?" I can't help giggling, and Ginny grins.

"It's something I do for free most of the time, so why not enjoy the benefits for a change?"

She lowers her voice and whispers, "Who knows, I may have unlocked a whole new business potentially."

Her sexy wink makes me laugh out loud and once again, I admire my friend. Ginny never has cared what anyone thinks of her and who wouldn't be impressed by that.

The show starts and we stare in delight at the fountain show with accompanying lights dancing on the lake to the sound of Whitney Houston. It's outstanding and I snap many photographs of the show reflected on the side of the Burj Khalifa. Home seems a million years away and for once I experience a freedom I haven't had for some time. It's addictive and the idea I had earlier hasn't been forgotten. If anything, it's growing out of control and being around my friends who reach out and grab life with both hands, makes me determined to do the same before it passes me by. The show is a backdrop to my expectations and cements my decision. Out with the old me and in with the new exciting vibrant woman who is about to step out of the shadows, a new one. All it has taken is a little of the magic of Dubai to rub off on me and determine my future self.

The show lasts for exactly four minutes, which surprises us all, and Sonia voices what the rest of us are thinking when she huffs, "Really. I thought it would last at least twenty minutes."

Ginny laughs. "It's not the length of time it takes, it's how amazing it is while it lasts that counts."

"Is that what Omar told you?" Amanda quips, causing us all to giggle like the Summerhouse girls we were many moons ago.

"Seriously though, Ginny, what the hell are you playing at?"

Sonia doesn't mince her words and Ginny says defensively, "Living my best life. You should know a lot about that, Sonia. You've been doing it since you left school."

The vitriol in her words stuns me a little and causes a nervous silence to push away the easy camaraderie of a few seconds ago and Sonia snaps, "You know nothing about my life."

Ginny merely shrugs. "I know you have a doting husband, two handsome boys, and a charmed existence."

I can barely look at Sonia because the mood has soured quicker than a cup of milk in the sun and Sonia snaps, "That came at a price."

Samantha catches my eye and I shrug imperceptibly as Sonia stops and says in a hurt voice, "If you must know, my life isn't quite the bed of roses you all think it is. Sometimes the blooms fade before eventually falling off, and Daniel isn't a saint by any stretch of the imagination. In fact..." She glares across at Samantha, who has turned deathly white and snaps, "You would know a lot about that, isn't that right, Samantha?"

Before she can say a thing, Sonia turns away and says with a sob. "I'm heading back to the hotel on the next bus. I've had enough."

We watch her walk away with stunned expressions and

then Amanda sighs and says apologetically, "I'm so sorry. She's been drinking all day and always gets a little emotional."

She glances at Sammy and smiles reassuringly. "It's ok. I'll go with her. Don't worry, she's just, well, a little over emotional right now."

As she walks away, Ginny and I glance at Sammy, who is staring after them in shock, and I say kindly, "Do you want to talk about that?"

Sammy shakes her head and says with confusion. "I don't know what she was talking about."

Ginny catches my eye, and it's obvious she's not buying it and I say brightly, "Perhaps we should leave Amanda to deal with Sonia and grab a drink in Starbucks. It's a shame to head back without seeing the rest of the mall, wouldn't you agree?"

Ginny nods and as we head back inside, it strikes me that maybe I'm not the only one hiding secrets beneath a crumbling surface.

15
SAMANTHA

I am actually shaking.

She knows.

It's taking every ounce of strength I possess to carry on as if nothing has happened because it's obvious Sonia knows it has.

I'm in shock, like a deer caught in headlights, and have an incredible urge to run. I never thought for one second Sonia knew about an event that will forever be my biggest mistake.

I'm grateful for my friend's support as they chatter between themselves, leaving me to gather my own horrified thoughts around me.

Sonia knows. But how?

I don't register the next two hours at all. I follow my friends around on autopilot, a thousand guilty thoughts crashing through my head as I work out what to say if Sonia confronts me. On the one hand, I always knew it would come out eventually and on the other, I hoped to avoid it. I swept it under the carpet with everything else I don't want to face in life and now Sonia has pulled that rug from under my feet.

When I think back to that time, I get palpitations. It was a dark interlude in my life that should never have happened. I have nobody to blame but myself, although Ben was really the catalyst responsible.

My heart lurches when I think of my errant husband and the pain that I've tried so hard to manage hits me hard. Will it ever go away? The desolation, the sense of loss and the pain of abandonment? It's been five years since he left, and I am no further forward now than I was then.

"Sammy." Catherine's gentle voice wafts into my ear and the tears build at the sympathy in her tone.

"I'm sorry." I blink away the tears and plaster a bright smile on my face as my two friends stare at me with concern.

"We were just saying we might head back, unless you haven't finished yet."

"No." I take a deep breath. "It's fine. I'm tired anyway and probably coming down with something."

The old excuse obviously doesn't cut it with my friends, and I turn away to avoid the questions in their eyes.

I'm not ready to open the can of worms Sonia's statement would cause, so I harden my heart and wrap my fingers around emotion and grip it firmly out of self-preservation.

We make the journey back, courtesy of the free shuttle bus, and I leave Catherine and Ginny to sit together, pretending to close my eyes in need of sleep. However, it's doubtful I will sleep tonight because if my dirty secret comes out, I can say goodbye to any friendships I have, and the last thirty years may as well be a fond memory.

I glance at the dazzling skyline as we drive through the energetic streets of Dubai. The sunshine has been replaced by artificial light and they burn brightly, twinkling around me like stars. Can I be happy here? Is it really an option, or just a pipe dream? It may be the answer to everything and renting an apartment and continuing my business halfway across the world may just keep my problem away for a little longer.

As we head back, I consider my plan and discover a new resolve. This is the answer. A brand-new life where nobody judges me. I can be anyone I want to be, and I definitely want to be somebody else right now. It's as if the stars have aligned and created an arrow pointing to the land of wealth and opportunity, and I would be a fool to ignore what fate has in store.

I just need to get through this trip and then I will be safe.

I am grateful for the bus journey to gather my thoughts and when we arrive back at the hotel, I face my friends with my shame firmly put back in its box.

"Nightcap anyone?" I smile and Ginny says with surprise, "I thought you weren't feeling well."

"Just a little tired, I guess. Maybe a medicinal brandy will help."

Ginny nods. "I'm up for that."

Catherine yawns loudly. "I'm not. I'm so tired I may not even make it up to my room before I fall asleep. Thanks for a great day, guys. I'll see you tomorrow."

She heads off and Ginny links her arm in mine.

"Come on. Let's add some more heat to the bill. I could use some alcohol. It's tough being in a country that frowns on it. I feel so guilty even asking for it, as if the alcohol police will pounce on me from the shadows and send me to a camp in the desert to clean up my act."

"You're such an idiot."

I roll my eyes as she grins. "A desperate idiot who would sleep with anyone who waved a bottle of Baileys in her face right now."

"Is that what Omar did, get you drunk in that lift before having his wicked way with you?"

Ginny winks. "You've got the wicked part right, but I was fully in control of all my faculties, and I will not make excuses for my sluttish behaviour other than he is incredibly gorgeous and I'm on holiday, so why not. Nobody was hurt."

I smile and turn away because as hard as I try, the guilt will never leave me and even innocent sentences like Ginny's remind me what a total bitch I am.

―――

We head to the bar on the fourth floor, and I absolutely adore the view. It's incredible, even at night and as we sit at a table under a heater, the candle flickering in a jar on the table, I could be forgiven for never wanting to leave.

Ginny also appears in a contemplative mood, and I decide to revisit the conversation we had in my room yesterday.

"Are you still thinking of moving here?" I ask, unsure of her response now she's had time to think about it.

"I've thought about it a lot. Have you?"

"Yes." I run my finger in an arc around my glass and sigh. "I really want to look into it. Ever since Ben left, life at home hasn't been the same."

"But that was ages ago." Ginny says in surprise, and I shrug.

"I hoped it would get better. It hasn't."

"Do you still see or hear from him?"

"Not directly, but I know everything I need to."

"Like what?" Ginny appears interested and I say wistfully, "I know he's engaged to Kate."

"You never said." Ginny's horrified gasp makes me chuck back the contents of the glass in one.

"Yes, a couple of years ago and they have twins now. Girls."

I fight back the tears as Ginny gasps. "But I always thought Ben didn't want children. You always told us that was the reason you never had any. That he was enough for you, and it was a mutual decision."

"I lied." I wipe the tears away that reveal my true emotion and Ginny's hand reaches across the table and grasps mine in a show of support.

"Do you want to talk about it?" I hear the same words for the second time today and this time I do.

"I loved him so much, Ginny." I stare at her with hurt abandonment. "He was everything to me and you remember how charming he is. He swept me off my feet and I would have agreed to any of his demands, no kids being one of them."

"One of them. You mean there were more, um, conditions?"

Ginny's horrified expression doesn't make me feel any better about how much of a doormat I became when it came to Ben and say sadly, "Yes. No kids, no mess, and no useless purchases. Everything in our home had to be in place, clean and orderly, and I suppose I always put that down to his military training. He was terribly OCD and would fly into a rage if things were out of place."

"I didn't realise."

Ginny looks concerned and I tap my fingers nervously on

the table as I voice something I have struggled so hard to contain.

"He was a bully, Ginny."

As I admit this out loud, it gives me a strength I wasn't expecting, and it doesn't seem as hard to say as I thought it would.

Ginny remains silent, and I test the water a little more.

"He would come home from work and fly into a rage if there was one thing out of place and if the dinner wasn't ready, or at least imminent. He made me feel worthless, like the most terrible wife on the planet, because I couldn't even perform the simplest tasks."

"The bastard." Ginny says through gritted teeth, and it makes me laugh.

"He was. Back then, anyway."

"What makes you say that?"

"I saw him once, a few months ago in town." My lip trembles as I remember a scene that made a mockery of my life with him.

"He was holding one of his girls on his shoulder and his fiancée Kate was holding the hand of the other girl, who didn't want to go in the pushchair. They were laughing and if there was ever an advert for the perfect family, they would have starred in it."

"That doesn't mean anything. Looks can be deceptive. You should know a lot about that." Ginny says kindly, but it's still brutal to hear.

"I guess, although they did look happy."

I stare out across the skyline and sigh. "I'm ashamed to admit I followed them for a bit. I was curious, and the fact I hoped to see the cracks appear tells me what a bitch I am."

"You're not a bitch; far from it." Ginny smiles, but I disagree.

"They went into a toy shop, and I watched them. Ben obviously adores his girls and helped them select a toy each. Kate was telling him off and he just hugged her and kissed her in full view of everyone and smiled. It broke my heart, Ginny, because he *never* looked at me like that."

"Not even at the beginning?"

"No. He said he loved me but never as if he really meant it. I suppose he always made me feel lucky that he picked me, and I did feel lucky. I mean, you met him. He's gorgeous, and that hasn't changed."

"Oh, Sammy." Ginny shakes her head. "I'm so sorry."

"What about?"

"Everything really. Obviously, you're still hurting, and Sonia was a bitch to use your situation and throw it back in your face back there at the mall. How could she compare your relationship to hers? It was cruel."

I stare at her in shock as she says angrily. "We all heard how Daniel cheated on her once but there was no need to drag your own experience into it. The fact it only happened with his secretary as a one off doesn't even compare to what you went through. I must say, she has sunk even lower in my estimation if I'm honest."

I hate that I say nothing. I hate that she's right in a way, and I hate that I am no better than Daniel.

With a deep sigh, I push the glass away and say wearily, "I'm heading off to bed. Tomorrow is another day and I intend on grabbing some sun while I can and think more about our plan to move here. It would be great to share an apartment and I'm sure it would be easy to bring both our businesses with us and set them up here. I'll look into it."

Ginny nods and as we head back to the lift, she links her arm in mine and says sweetly, "I've got your back, Sammy.

Whatever happens, I'll always be on your side. You can rely on me."

Once again, the tears build as she reminds me of what a fantastic friend she is and always has been. Ginny may be many things, but her loyalty is never in question, and I can't think of anyone I would rather reinvent myself with than her.

16

GINNY

I feel so sorry for Samantha. We all thought she hit the jackpot when she met Ben, which shows me how foolish we were. None of us questioned their relationship all the time they were together, even though in hindsight, she never appeared gloriously happy.

I always put it down to the fact that Ben was away a lot, and she was probably fearful that he wouldn't make it back. Their life together consisted of endless tours of duty and many goodbyes. It must have been hard not knowing if he would be coming back alive, or in a Union Jack flag-draped casket.

I never for one moment thought he was mentally abusing

her. Coercive control is an actual crime these days and yet, from her description, he is a different person entirely with his new younger fiancée. I hurt for my friend and probably for the first time, congratulate myself on my own choices in life. I never married and have none of the guilt or baggage that my friends appear to drag behind them like chains around their soul.

I reach my room and as soon as I enter, I wonder if I'm in the wrong one because it's filled entirely with red roses.

I blink in surprise as I register the glorious blooms in vases on every surface. There are rose petals on the bed and a huge heart made from roses on a stand positioned by the window.

I am stunned as the powerful scent hits me, and the tears fall as I am completely blown away by such an extravagant gesture.

For a moment, I sit on the edge of the bed in a trance and then reach for my phone and stare at Omar's number in an indecisive second before I press dial on FaceTime.

My heart flutters mercilessly as he answers the call and just seeing his handsome face causes the longing to shoot through my entire body.

"My darling, what a pleasant surprise." He says in that husky voice that melts every doubt I own.

"Omar." I smile nervously. "Did you send me flowers?" I arch my brow and he chuckles. "A few."

I scan the phone around the room and then stare back at him. "Why? It's well, a little over the top, wouldn't you agree?"

"No." He shrugs and as he pulls the phone back, I catch a

glimpse of his tanned ripped chest in all its naked splendour and my mouth waters at the silk pants that hang low on his hips. It appears I've interrupted his sleep because he rakes his fingers through his jet-black hair and the stubble on his jaw is seriously messing with my libido right now.

His dark, sexy eyes gaze back at me sleepily and he twists his lips into a mischievous grin and whispers, "Nothing is too much for you, my darling. Let me spoil you."

"Why?" I am genuinely confused because this is starting to concern me a lot and he shrugs, licking his lips before saying huskily, "Don't question a gift, Ginny. It's not good manners."

It makes me laugh out loud. "There is usually an occasion attached to gift giving. What's this one?" I say with a smile, and he grins.

"New beginnings."

I settle back against the bed and drown in the vista before me. It's as if every wish I ever had is being granted to me in this magical place and, of course, I doubt every sweet gesture he's making. However, I can't deny the attraction I have for this man and it's not because of the gifts he is lavishing on me, and I say softly, "I missed you today."

"Me too."

He grins and I whisper, "How was your business meeting?"

"Routine."

"Did you get what you needed?" I'm not sure why I am even asking, but I expect it's to form a picture of the man who has crashed into my life so suddenly.

"I always get what I want, my darling. You will soon understand that."

"Does that apply to me?" His words make me nervous

because they imply he has yet to get what he wants from me, despite how freely I gave myself to him.

"Of course."

"Then tell me." I hold my breath waiting for the reason the genie from my Aladdin's lamp is in control of my life, and he chuckles softly.

"You are curious, mistrusting even, and I understand why."

"You do?"

He nods. "You are searching for a reason why I am spoiling you. An ulterior motive that would form the plot of many thrillers on Netflix."

"Are you?" I grin and he laughs out loud, before saying in a sexy whisper, "I live a lonely life, Ginny, and I think you know a lot about how that feels. I move from country to country and never stay long enough to put down roots. I get my kicks from chance encounters and enjoy them while they last before moving onto the next one. I earn more money than I can spend, so I enjoy spoiling the women in my life."

"The women?" I knew there was a catch and I feel like a fool as I face the conclusion that I'm one in a very long line.

"Woman." He says huskily and whispers, "One woman at a time. No cheating and no messing around. I will not lie and say I haven't slept with hundreds of women; I have."

I'm not feeling any better about this, as he says with a sigh. "All the time they are happy I treat them like queens. It only changes when they grow tired of the nature of our relationship. You see, Ginny..."

He sits up, his back against the ornate headboard, and stares darkly into the camera.

"I am never around long enough to form a meaningful relationship. Women want more of my time, commitment, a family, and a ring on their left finger. I can't commit to that, so I leave and move onto the next challenge."

"So, it's just sex." I hold my breath and he says huskily, "Lots of it when we meet and, if you agree to my lifestyle, there are trips abroad, holidays and meals in the finest restaurants. It's not always sex, but companionship too. Every date is treated like a first date and some women find that hard to deal with."

He glances at the gold Rolex on his wrist and says firmly, "I need to sleep. I have an important meeting in the morning. We will continue this conversation when we catch up in London. If you agree to my terms, then we enjoy a satisfying relationship. If you can't, we walk away with no hard feelings involved."

"I'll think about it."

I say the words, but I already know my answer because who wants commitment, anyway? I mean, he promised never to cheat, so surely this is the perfect situation. A rich man who is everything I ever wanted, just not sharing my address and someone I don't have to cook and clean for. I'm happy to sign up for something that has my demands written all over it and so I smile and blow him a kiss and whisper, "Sleep tight, gorgeous stranger."

I cut the call before he can reply and smile to myself as I gaze around the room at the florist's windfall. What's so bad about this, anyway? It's a gift that will keep on giving and I would be a fool to walk away from an experience I am never likely to forget.

17
AMANDA

Sonia ranted about our friends for the entire journey home, and it took all my strength not to bite. When she's had a few too many cocktails, her aggression comes out to play and it was lucky we left the others back at the mall.

As soon as we reached the hotel, Sonia stormed off to our room and grabbed a bottle of prosecco from the insanely expensive mini bar and said petulantly, "I'm going to bed with the only company I need right now."

As the door slammed behind her, it left me at peace for the first time since we arrived.

Finally, I can relax knowing she will probably pass out and wake up with no knowledge of this in the morning.

I shower and change into my loungewear and take my phone onto the balcony with a coffee I made from the machine in our room. Despite being close to ten pm, it's only five pm at home and I have an overwhelming desire to speak to my mother.

"Hey, you look tired, my girl. Have you been drinking again?"

Mum says as soon as she answers, and I grin, loving seeing her friendly face, courtesy of FaceTime.

"Not really, but it is bedtime here."

"Of course." Mum smiles. *"Are you having fun?"*

"Yes, thanks. How are things there?"

She shrugs. *"Quiet."*

"Where is everyone?"

"Freddie's at a friend's house, some guy called Marcus."

"That's normal." I laugh because Freddie and Marcus could be twins who were separated at birth. If he's not there, Marcus is at our house, and they are probably playing computer games as normal.

Mum carries on. *"India is in her room. She says she must study, but she's been in there for hours already."*

"She does that." It makes me laugh. "She probably *is* studying. She's just like her father. They get lost in what they're doing and forget the time."

Mum laughs. *"You've got that right. Anyway, this home resembles a hotel. Jasper left at four am and told me he would be back around ten. Is that normal, or is because we're here?"*

She sounds a little hurt and I say gently, "Usual, I'm afraid. I'm a banking widow for five days a week and at the weekend he spends most of his time catching up with everything he couldn't fit in during the week."

"I don't know how you put up with it."

Mum shakes her head in disapproval, and I say quickly, "What about Saskia?"

"She went out with a friend to watch another one in a show."

"That will be Millie. She's at the Brit school and is always performing somewhere."

Mum laughs. *"I'm a little redundant if I'm honest. I doubt they even realise I'm here."*

"Now you know how I feel." I make a joke of it, but it's there deep inside me. The knowledge I am no longer required, and it hurts – a lot.

"So, tell me about Dubai. Is it magical?"

"Magical?" I laugh. "I suppose, although Sonia appears to have drunk all the magic and is now probably passed out in her room."

"Still the same, then." Mum purses her lips and shakes her head. *"She should seek help for that 'problem' she has."*

I nod. "I agree. Maybe I can persuade her while I'm here."

"You're a good friend, Amanda."

"If you say so." I sigh and glance at the Cartier watch Jasper bought me, sparkling in the dusky light.

"I'm heading off to bed. Night mum and thanks."

"I love you, darling. Enjoy yourself, you deserve it."

As I cut the call, it's with tears in my eyes. I deserve it, she says. Do I? I'm not sure I really deserve any of what I have because it's all there by accident of marriage.

When have I ever worked hard in my life? Never. There are many people in the line before me who deserve a break like this, and I am definitely not one of them. I do what every other mother does. Care for her family, wash, cook and clean and make my husband's life easier while he provides it all. Am I happy? Not really, and am I ungrateful? Never. I am *always* grateful, which is probably half the problem. I never really found Amanda Donovan and what she wanted from life. I thought I did, but now that reason is drifting away, I need to form a new one.

What does the future hold for a banking widow whose children are about to fly the nest? What happens when my husband retires, and I discover we have nothing in common after all? Life is changing quicker than I can deal with, and I'm unsure of the future. Is Sonia right and I am the lucky one? I wish it felt like that.

A sudden need to connect with my husband overwhelms me and against my better judgement, I reach for my phone. Despite the fact Jasper hates to be interrupted at work and detests FaceTime, I have an overwhelming desire to see him.

I almost think he's not going to answer, but just as I hover over the 'end' button, his tired face fills my screen.

"Is there a problem?"

My heart lurches as I smile nervously. "No. I just missed you."

"Oh."

I don't miss the spark of irritation in his eyes before he says with a sigh. *"It's crazy here."*

I peer past him and see the monitors scrolling haphazardly and say apologetically, "I know you hate to be interrupted, but well, it's strange being here without you."

His expression softens, and he smiles. *"I miss you too."*

For some reason, that is enough for me, which shows how messy our marriage is now. He glances behind him and sighs heavily. *"I should get back to it. Enjoy your break, darling. Buy yourself a memento in the mall. That should make you happy."*

He grins and then blows me a kiss before saying quickly, *"See you when you get home. Love you."*

A blank screen receives my own response and I die a little inside. I feel like a selfish bitch because I'm unhappy with my life. Who wouldn't be happy? Jasper devotes his time and attention to making money to keep us in comfort. To educate our children in the best way we can and provide us with an amazing home and no financial worries. Why do I want more than that?

I've concluded that the most important things in life cost nothing except thought and time. I am a poor recipient of that and buying the latest designer handbag or driving away from the showroom in a new custom-made car, holds none of the thrill that a simple loving act would have. I want my husband to give me some attention and that costs nothing at all.

As I curl up in the huge king size bed alone, I could well be at home because there is always a cold empty space beside me. Jasper often sleeps in one of the spare bedrooms if he gets home late and leaves early, which is increasingly more often these days. Unlike Sonia, I don't worry that he's having an affair because the only mistress in his life is the Stock Exchange. Will he burn out before I get my husband back, a shell of the person he was when I married him? Will we have things in common because aside from the kids, we don't? Should I insist on his attention, or should I just bide my time, patiently waiting for my husband to notice me again?

18

AMANDA

Waking up in Dubai is something I could never tire of. The fact the sun shines all year round and the temperature is a comfortable thirty degrees, I would be a fool not to love it.

I pull on a maxi dress and wait patiently for Sonia to surface while I sip a cold juice from the minibar on the balcony overlooking the water.

The city in the distance provides a surreal backdrop against the private sandy beach that every hotel on the palm enjoys as standard.

I wasn't joking when I said I was missing Jasper. I would

give anything to be here with him, despite how much I enjoy spending time with my friends.

A loud groan behind me alerts me to the waking beast inside my best friend and I smile with concern. "How did you sleep?"

Sonia heads onto the balcony, looking as if she hardly slept at all, the bags under them heavier than the designer ones she carried back from the mall, revealing the effects of alcohol and probably little sleep.

"I hate the bed, it's so uncomfortable." She says with an irritated sigh. "Thomas called and asked if I had left anything for dinner because the fridge was empty."

I stifle a grin because like me, Sonia is responsible for every meal, packed lunch, and item of clothing our kids need, and we are always receiving calls and texts asking where something is.

She slumps into the seat opposite and says a little shakily, "I asked where Daniel was, and he said he wasn't home yet."

"Working I guess." I reassure her and she nods, appearing deep in thought as she glances across the skyline.

"Do you think..."

"Don't."

"What?" she says with irritation, and I say as reassuringly as I can. "Don't overthink it. There is no reason to believe Daniel is anywhere but at work."

"That's easy for you to say. Jasper never goes anywhere else."

Her words burn, but I brush them off as I always do.

"True, and Daniel is no different. If anything, he is working extra hard because he's just started."

Once again, Daniel is a new starter because he never shaped up in his old company and switched to a lower grade job with a less illustrious one.

Sonia shrugs. "Which brings with it new opportunities and not of the financial kind either."

Her tone is bitter, and I feel a surge of sympathy for my oldest friend. It's one thing fighting against a profession, but another thing entirely when you're fighting against another human being. Daniel has always been attracted to the chase, and he chases a lot. Sonia is a saint for putting up with it over the years and I'd hoped Daniel would calm down the older he got. If anything, he's got worse and I say tentatively, "Have you ever considered leaving him?"

Sonia shrugs. "All the time, but where would I go?"

"Nowhere. He would give you the house."

"And what would I run it on? Unlike you, I don't have savings or a bottomless credit card. Knowing you, Jasper has deposited the maximum amount in every ISA going and maxed out the premium bond allowance in your name. It's ok for you, we have nothing."

She ignores my horrified expression and sighs heavily.

"If we separated, he would insist on selling the house and dividing the proceeds fifty-fifty. He would carry on working and living the lifestyle he aspires to, and I would be searching for jobs with no experience other than being a doormat for my entire life. No, leaving Daniel isn't an option I'm willing to cash in and so, as always, I'll wait for his latest craze to fizzle out and hope his libido crashes and he can't get it up anymore."

She stares around her and says with a sigh. "Perhaps Ginny had the right idea all along. Stay free and independent and focus entirely on herself. I always thought she was selfish and rather lonely as it happens but watching her seizing the moment with that handsome stranger has made me doubt every decision I've ever made in my life."

"That's quite some statement." I say in awe and Sonia

shrugs. "Maybe it's not too late after all. I could meet my own rich Arab, who will show me how a woman should be treated. What do you say, Amanda? We've done it once. This could be history repeating itself."

"You marry for love, and you stay married to make that decision the right one."

She shakes her head. "I guess you're right. If I gave it up, gave Daniel up, it would be admitting I made the biggest mistake of my life and I don't make mistakes — ever."

She winks and stands, a little of the old Sonia flashing before my eyes.

"Come on. Let's go and eat before tanning for the day. I can't waste any more time worrying about Daniel and what he may be doing when I am thinking along those same lines myself."

As we leave the room, I realise she is only saying it. Sonia is besotted with her husband and always has been. He can do no wrong in her eyes and I suppose she does stay with him rather than admit she made a mistake. Appearances have always been the number one rule she lives by and outwardly portrays an enviable life that most women would kill for. The trouble is the person she's killing is herself because love turned to bitterness years ago.

———

Catherine is waiting and smiles sweetly as we sit down.

"Another glorious day in paradise." She grins as we take our seats opposite, side by side, as we always have.

"What happened after we left?" I say curiously and she shrugs. "We grabbed a drink and made it back not long after you. Samantha and Ginny had a nightcap, but I was so tired I turned in for the night."

As she speaks, I notice several texts lighting up her phone and I say with a smile, "Somebody wants your attention."

"Lucky you." Sonia grumbles and as Catherine raises her eyes, I shake my head imperceptibly.

Sonia scrapes back her chair and says with a sigh, "I'm grabbing something from the buffet, are you coming?"

"No. I'll drink my tea first but go ahead."

As she leaves, Catherine says with concern. "What was that about yesterday?"

"What?"

"Sonia's remark to Samantha."

"I don't know, probably nothing."

"It upset her."

"What did she say?"

I'm as intrigued as Catherine because I didn't think anything about it and merely put it down to Sonia making it all about her as usual.

"It was in poor taste if you ask me. I mean, referring to Samantha's own humiliation when Ben was cheating on her. Sonia was out of order."

Something is telling me that wasn't her intention at all, which makes me wonder about the meaning of the remark. From her reaction it appeared more personal than that and yet I brush it aside as the woman herself hurries back to the table holding a plate loaded with pastries.

"Comfort food." She mumbles as she begins shovelling a pain-au-chocolate into her mouth, and I don't miss the concern on Catherine's face as Ginny drops down beside her.

"Well, isn't this a beautiful morning?"

She beams and I grin, glad that at least one of us is happy.

"How was your evening?"

I enquire, and she smiles with the smugness of someone who has everything worked out.

"I called Omar and demanded to know what his intentions are."

"Wow, Ginny, I'm impressed." Sonia says with her mouth full.

"Yes. I asked him outright what was going on and he told me he just wanted to spoil his woman and for as long as I want it to be, that woman is now me."

"He said that." Catherine's eyes are wide and Ginny grins. "He told me he was lonely and never has the opportunity to meet someone and settle down. Women get possessive and demand more of his time, which is a luxury he doesn't have."

I wonder why the warning bells are deafening me right now because Ginny just described my own situation in one smug sentence.

"And you're happy with that. A few snatched moments in between business trips?" I must ask, and she nods. "Why not? I'm a busy woman. I have a business too, which I may relocate out here, by the way."

"What?"

Sonia looks up in shock and Ginny nods. "Yes, Samantha is of the same mind, and we may rent an apartment and chance things over here. Omar could visit when he's in town and sometimes I could travel with him when I have a free week or so. It's exciting, don't you think?"

We all fall silent because it sounds like an impossible dream, for those with ties, anyway, and yet I'm guessing that every one of the three women listening would trade places with Ginny in a heartbeat if we were in her position.

Samantha joins us and I don't miss the hesitant glance she throws Sonia's way and takes the seat beside Ginny and smiles shakily. "Morning guys, sorry I'm late."

"We never set a time." Sonia dismisses her with a wave and scrapes back her seat again. "Amanda, you haven't eaten anything yet. Come and help me decide on pancakes or a full English."

Sighing inside, I join my friend, used to being at her beck and call all my life and yet as I walk away, it's with severe envy accompanying me because Ginny is living the dream right now and if I'm jealous of anyone, it's her.

19
CATHERINE

I can't wait until breakfast is over. It was difficult to ignore the texts coming through as if they were normal because my phone is quieter than a graveyard most days. I can't believe this is happening so quickly, and I am excited to retreat to my personal space and pore over the messages.

I'm the first one to make my excuses and leave the others to head back to dip into my guilty secret in the solitude of my room.

As soon as I reach its sanctuary, I kick off my shoes and jump onto the bed, interested in seeing the results of my sinful act.

Last night I went to bed earlier than Ginny and Samantha for a very good reason. To set up my profile on DateApp, which is a site for women approaching a certain age and is perfect for my purposes. I used a pseudonym because the last thing I need is anyone discovering what I'm up to, especially Connor and God forbid, Sally. I took the free option for now because if I want the detailed service, I need to upload a driving licence to prove I'm genuine.

However, I am just testing the water and so I peer eagerly at my screen, noting with some satisfaction I have received fifteen notifications.

If I am holding on to any guilt that I'm cat-fishing these people, I soon discard it like an old rag when I see the photographs of the men who, as the younger generation would say, have slid into my DMs.

To be honest, I never expected them to be so attractive and I stare in amazement at my wish list appearing in human form before my eyes. The fact my own profile picture is off a stock image site doesn't concern me because this is more fun than I've had in years.

I told myself I would have some fun with it and then delete it from my phone before I get home. Connor will never find out, and I will have restored my self-confidence knowing I have other options.

Quite a few, apparently and as I scroll through the messages, it gives me pleasure because I feel wanted for a change.

I make sure to respond to every single one out of politeness more than anything, and yet one in particular has captured my attention because he appears to be everything I want in life.

Tall, dark, and handsome with a rugged complexion that tells me he is no office worker. He is pictured with a black

Labrador and his open, honest face makes me smile. Most of his photographs are in gorgeous landscapes and a few by the pool on one of his holidays. Unlike my own pretend profile picture, I have given nothing else away, which probably screams imposter to every potential match who comes across it.

I don't know why I thought this would work really, but curiosity gets the better of me and so I tentatively type out a rather flirty text back to Jack Bennett because so far, he's perfect.

I join the others by the pool and feel different somehow.

As if I could conquer the world which obviously shows because Sonia says grumpily, "I don't know why you're looking so happy."

There's an awkward silence and I say cagily, "Why wouldn't I be happy? Look where we are. This could be paradise."

"For some maybe."

Sonia turns over to tan her back and Amanda shakes her head before throwing me a sympathetic smile.

Ginny, however, has never been one to mince her words and has obviously had enough of the tense atmosphere, which is entirely of Sonia's making and says in a firm voice, "OK, I've had enough of this. What's going on, Sonia, and don't fob us off because we've known you too long for that?"

I swear even the pool stops rippling as we all stare at Sonia in shock, wondering what she's going to say about this intrusion and, to our surprise, she just sits up and shakes her head mournfully.

"Is it really that obvious?"

"Yes." A collective answer shows we're all on the same page and she sighs a little sheepishly.

"I suppose you should know, although I'd hoped to keep

it quiet until we got back. This is supposed to be a celebration, after all. I mean, it's not every day we turn fifty and just because I'm the first one in the line, you're not far behind me."

She sits up and pulls her shades over her eyes, effectively disguising her expression, and appears a little unsure which has got to be a first.

"Go on." Amanda encourages her and Sonia shrugs before saying emotionlessly, "Before we came away, Daniel told me that one of his property investment portfolios had crashed and the investors have lost everything."

Ginny says in confusion, "Why is that a bad thing for you, for us even?"

An icy hand claws at my heart as her gaze falls on me and I can tell it's not due to sunburn that her face is so red.

"I'm sorry, guys, it was the Hades consortium."

My earlier euphoria evaporates quicker than a droplet of water in the desert sun because what the actual fuck? We invested in that consortium because Sonia assured us it was a sure-fire way to double our investment inside a year.

There is silence as we take in the news and I'm more surprised when Ginny sobs, "Fuck!"

I stare at her in amazement as Sonia whispers, "I'm sorry, Ginny."

"Why?" I'm confused because surely, she should be apologising to me, not Ginny, but as our usually controlled friend breaks down before our eyes, the reality hits home.

"Ginny re-mortgaged her house to invest." Sonia offers by way of an explanation. Amanda looks horrified and Ginny sobs, "I can't believe I was so stupid. I've lost everything I worked so hard for."

Amanda shakes her head. "I don't understand."

Sonia says with a catch to her voice, "We told Ginny about

the investment opportunity, and she decided to buy in." She peers at me and says in a small voice. "You both did. I'm sorry."

This time their attention turns to me, and Ginny says with a break to her voice, "I'm sorry, Catherine."

The fact Connor couldn't wait to invest tells me Karma's a bitch and I'm not nearly as concerned as my friend because Connor only invested the contents of one his ISAs.

"It's ok. I don't think we'll be affected other than a blow to Connor's pride and an ISA account."

The fact Sonia appears even more uncomfortable puts me on edge and I say quickly, "What?"

"Is that what he told you?" Sonia says carefully and I nod, now extremely confused.

"Yes."

Sonia sighs and lowers her voice. "He invested two hundred thousand pounds."

"I'm sorry." I'm not sure if I heard her right, and she nods miserably.

"He told Daniel it was too much of a gift not to open and piled your life savings into it."

"But we still have the house — don't we?"

My mind is spinning as I grasp at everything we've built up in the hope of saving it and Sonia shrugs. "You'll have to ask him that question."

I feel sick and whisper, "Does Connor know?"

"They have a meeting today. He soon will."

I slump back against my seat, my mind racing, and Ginny says with a tremor to her voice, "Is there any way out of this mess?"

Sonia shrugs. "Daniel's working on it."

She turns to Amanda. "He told me he's going to ask Jasper for help. If anyone can help, he can."

From the look on Amanda's face, she's not happy about that and just nods, followed by a tight smile.

"Of course."

Samantha gasps, "I can't believe it. So, all of you have lost hundreds of thousands of pounds overnight because of a company going under. I don't understand. Weren't there any red flags, a warning perhaps?"

Our attention turns to Sonia, who can't even look at us, and then she sighs. "If you must know, Daniel's been working on it for the past month. He was certain he would get an investor and then it happened."

"What did?" Samantha says in horror and Sonia replies in a dull voice. "He told me a big investor had bought in and saved the project. There was enough money to finish the development, and it was back on track."

"So, what happened?" Ginny says with exasperation. "And why didn't Daniel tell us there were problems, anyway?"

"Because there are *always* problems when dealing with money."

Sonia snaps. "Tell her Amanda. It's why they are paid so well because millions could be lost overnight with no warning, and they must be on it the entire time just to keep the balls in the air."

"That Daniel has dropped several times now." Ginny says nastily and I can tell this conversation is about to descend into chaos, so I say loudly, "Let's not argue about what should have happened. Let's talk about what *is* happening."

I turn to Sonia. "So, this meeting. What's it about?"

Sonia glances down and says nervously. "It's to pull the plug on it and accept it's over."

"But you said they had a large investor. What happened to their money?" I say in disbelief, and Sonia shrugs. "Apparently, they invested heavily, which drove the share price up and then sold, causing it to crash."

"Who are they?"

Sonia shrugs. "A company that is beyond reproach. Like most people, they were just playing the markets and had a good reason why they were pulling out."

"What good reason?" Ginny fumes. "I thought there were laws against this kind of thing."

I notice Sonia wince as she says quickly. "They discovered the site was of archaeological interest. When they were digging, they found the remains of a settlement dating from before the birth of Christ. That was it. The diggers were stopped immediately."

"Did the investor know about that?" I say, more from curiosity than anything. It's almost as if I'm so far removed from the situation it's happening to someone else.

"They say not, but you never can tell when money is concerned." Sonia answers.

"But the land is still ours." Ginny says quickly, "We still own a valuable asset."

"You don't." Sonia snaps. "You were part owner of a development that never got off the ground. No development, no investment and all you have are worthless shares in a company that is currently being liquidised along with all the assets it has, i.e. your money is being used to pay off people they owe."

As the reality settles around us like a dark cloud over the sun, everything changes in an instant. Life as we know it has become something else entirely, and it's not so certain anymore. Being so far away from home is a godsend really because after that meeting today, my life wouldn't be worth living because Connor hates to lose a penny from his pocket, let alone everything we have worked so hard to build.

20

SONIA

I'm shaking inside. I knew when I dropped this bombshell the fallout was likely to be severe, but I never really expected to feel as if I just killed my whole family.

After much discussion, we all retreated to our rooms to lick our wounds and I'm grateful for the space so I can process what happened.

They hate me. It was flashing in their eyes like a hazard warning light. I don't blame them. Not really, and yet if the investment had worked, they would be thanking me and singing my praises.

With a sigh as deep as the middle of the ocean, I head

towards the mini bar and retrieve the bottle of gin I brought with me from Duty Free. This time I unscrew the cap and forego the glass because my need is too great to wait.

As the alcohol erases a little of the pain, I collect my tortured thoughts and wander across to the balcony. A serene scene of decadence and privilege winks back at me and I wonder when living life to this standard became so important to me.

All my life, I've perfected a façade that I present to the world. Successful, in control, and confident. It's served me well over the years and taken me to a place I never deserved. Not really. I was average at school yet managed to convince everyone I was capable. I mixed with the right crowd and was the model student. It worked well and I was expected to do well. It was a given that Sonia Batchelor would do very well in life, and I did.

I married Daniel, who was of a similar mind to me and between us we carved out a place for ourselves in society. Occasionally, that place has been under threat, but we always managed to pull it back.

I wonder if that will be possible this time.

Fear is not a pleasant emotion to experience, and I've nurtured it inside me my entire life. Fear of being discovered as the charlatan I really am.

Witnessing my friend's anguish first-hand was an unexpected pain I never expected. They knew the score. Didn't they? Investments are risky, I know a lot about that, but it didn't make me feel any better knowing I was the messenger of some life destroying news.

One more swig of Dutch courage will be all it takes to tidy the shelf in my mind. Get everything in order so I can deal with this latest setback.

As the burn coats me inside it gives me confidence and taking out my phone, I call the man who never fails to disappoint me every single time.

"Sonia. How did it go?"

"Badly." I snap as I settle down on the bed and prepare to listen to more bad news.

"What about your end? How did Connor take it?"

"Angry, as expected."

"Understandable."

Daniel sighs heavily and says with an urgent whisper, *"Listen. I don't suppose you could sweet-talk Amanda for me."*

My heart sinks.

"How?"

He answers with a catch in his voice, *"I need to ask Jasper for help."*

"Then ask him." I'm a little irritated that any conversation between Jasper and Daniel usually happens after I instigate it.

"He's not returning my calls."

My jaw drops because this is a first and I say quickly, "How many calls have you made?"

"Ten." He says angrily. *"I've left texts, voicemails and even been around there, but all I found was Amanda's mum and the gardener."*

"What? Together!" I'm hoping for some form of scandal to detract from mine, and he growls, *"Don't be stupid. Of course they weren't together."*

My anger is almost at boiling point because if anyone's stupid, it's the waste of talent I married and I snap, "Don't speak to me like that. I never got us into this mess, but as always, it's up to me to sort it."

There's a brief silence before he says with a groan.

"Organise a meal with them when you get back. Make it for the next evening. I'll corner him then."

"I'll try." I sigh heavily. "This is the last time, Daniel. I mean it."

"Of course, this is the last time. We were just unlucky."

I think back on the many other times we were unlucky and can only find one common denominator and it's the man on the other end of the phone.

I wonder when the gin bottle became more attractive to me than my husband, quite some time ago I think and so I say sharply, "I've got to go. I'll see you tomorrow."

"Yes, have a safe flight and um, Sonia…"

"What?"

"Don't spend any more money. We can't afford it."

His words come at me like a bolt of lightning from out of nowhere and I gasp, "What do you mean?"

I don't like the silence on the other end of the phone before he says with an obvious lump in his throat. *"Our assets have been frozen, pending an investigation."*

"What investigation? What have you done, Daniel?"

"Just normal procedure and nothing to worry about but well, keep off the credit card and reduce your spending to well, um zero if you can."

I am stunned and lost for words as he forces some brightness into his voice and says quickly, *"I should go. An email's come through I need to answer. I'll see you tomorrow."*

He cuts the call abruptly, leaving me feeling even worse than before the call.

I take a moment for the news to sink in. We have nothing left. In fact, we have a huge problem by the sound of it because it appears that Daniel is in more trouble than he's letting on. I can tell when he's lying to me and even halfway across the world, I sensed it. Something is about to change, and I'm guessing the cosy bubble we live inside is about to explode, scattering what's left of our comfortable life into the gutter, where we'll tumble in after it.

21

SONIA

The empty gin bottle lies discarded in the bin, and I toss some paperwork I no longer need from the flight on top of it.

If anything, I am numb inside, something the gin is good at creating.

My mind is foggy, which I largely put down to the menopause, but in truth alcohol has been propping me up for some time now.

I zip my case shut and stare at the bulging suitcase and wonder when I'll use it again. What will happen when we return home, and will I ever enjoy a shopping spree again?

As I pick up the designer handbag and wind the Hermes scarf around my neck, I fight back the tears.

Fifty and foolish. That's me and now I must endure a few more hours apologising to my friends before I can shut myself away in the sanctuary of my home while my husband digs us out of the mess he created.

Amanda knocks on the door and from the expression on her face, I can tell something has happened and for a brief moment I hope she is suffering as much as I am. Perhaps the reason Jasper never called Daniel is that he is fighting for survival too, and my heart leaps at the thought that someone else will be going through the same drama as I am.

"I can't find my purse."

Amanda shakes her head in obvious distress. "I last saw it in the mall."

"It must be somewhere." I say, blinking in astonishment, and she says sharply, "I've looked everywhere. In fact, I've turned the room upside down and it now looks as if I've been burgled. Should I call the police?"

"What can they do?"

I really don't have time to deal with Amanda's problems as well as my own and she says tightly, "I just wondered if you'd seen it."

"Well, I haven't. Go and search again. It's probably under a piece of furniture or something."

She leaves and I don't miss the frown that goes with her, but I can't worry about what Amanda's thinking. My problems are far greater than a lost purse and so I haul my case to the floor and stare around me with a sinking feeling inside. This may be the last time I ever see a hotel suite as extravagant as this one is. Heavy blue silk curtains spun with gold edging. A matching bed cover and scatter cushions that complement it perfectly. Every inch of the room drips opulence from the soft carpet to the twinkling chandelier hanging from the moulded rose in the centre of the room.

Brilliant sunshine pours inside and lights every corner, making everything appear fantastic. This is the life I always deserved and, for the most part, achieved until my foolish husband ruined everything.

After one last lingering look around, I head into the small living area that separates our room and leaving my cases for the butler to transport to our waiting minibus, I head into Amanda's room and find her zipping up her own case.

"Did you find it?"

"No." She shrugs. "I've been through everything and still nothing. It must have been stolen at the mall."

"Unlikely."

She says rather grumpily, "Why not?"

"Because there is no crime in Dubai, and nobody would steal a purse out of fear of being arrested. You know that because the cab driver who brought us here told us so."

"So, it must have fallen out. Possibly it was handed in."

"There is no time to retrace our steps, though." I say sharply, and Amanda nods with a big sigh. "I guess so."

Then she throws another grenade into the room and says apologetically, "I'm afraid you'll have to pick up the bill. My credit cards were in my purse, and I have no way of paying it."

"I'm sorry, what?" I stare at her in disbelief, and she shrugs. "Just put it on your credit card and I'll settle up with you as soon as we get home."

I swear the blood rushes to my head, and I'm convinced detonates a panic attack.

"Are you kidding me?"

"Of course not. Do you have a problem with that?"

Her sharp stare causes me to colour up and I stumble over my words.

"I'm not sure if I've got enough credit on my card."

She shrugs. "I'm sure it will be fine."

She appears thoughtful and then says with a wave of her hand. "There was also the meal we had in the a la carte restaurant before the others got here. Oh, and the hair appointment in the hotel salon. I'm not sure if the manicure was included in that, but it shouldn't come to a lot. You'll be fine."

A growing sense of panic is making me regret emptying the gin bottle already and if it wasn't for the fact it would add more to the bill, I would be draining the last dregs of alcohol from my mini bar. Before I can answer, a gentle knock on the door alerts us to the butler calling and Amanda says brightly, "It will be fine. Just a minor inconvenience that will be resolved when we return home."

As she opens the door, the butler heads inside, closely followed by the man in charge of removing our cases. I follow Amanda in a daze because how am I going to explain if my credit card isn't up to the job?

As we walk through the corridors, my mind is buzzing with possibilities of ways I can avoid an unpleasant situation and as Amanda presses for the lift, it hits me in a eureka moment.

I say quickly, "I think I've forgotten my passport. You head down and I'll meet you in reception."

Amanda nods as the lift doors close behind her and as soon as I'm free of her piercing glare, I spin on my heels and head to the room of the only person who can help me right now.

22

SAMANTHA

Normally when I leave to return home after a pleasant trip, I'm dreading it. This time, however, I'm excited because it's organising my return. The more time I've spent here, the more at home I am, and I am certain it is the right decision to make. To relocate my business away from the painful memories back at home. A fresh start and a new beginning and who better than to do it with than one of my oldest friends?

I've already searched for apartments to rent and checked up on the working rules for non-nationals and I really believe I can make this work.

I am so excited because for the first time in my life I am

doing something off centre and unexpected. I will no longer look over my shoulder when I'm out in town, in fear of seeing Ben with his new family. I will be scripting my own future without him in it and, who knows, hopefully find somebody new. Somebody successful like Ginny's Omar, or even just someone kind. Dubai will be the perfect place for my brave new world, and I am impatient to return home and set the wheels in motion.

As I tug my case to the ground, a gentle knock on the door makes me jump and as I head over to answer it, I'm surprised to see Sonia standing there regarding me with a strange expression.

"Are you ok?" I ask nervously because she appears angry about something and I'm even more surprised when she pushes her way into the room and slams the door behind her.

"I know, Samantha." She wastes no time in saying angrily.

"I don't understand. What?"

I am genuinely confused and then she whips the rug out from under my feet and snaps, "That you had an affair with my husband."

I step back in shock, all my demons circling, no longer hidden and swirling around me as they delight in my moment of shame.

"How?" I gasp, the tears welling up in my eyes as Sonia says angrily, "Daniel told me. He couldn't live with the guilt and told me you had been pestering him."

"He said what?" I'm aghast, and she points her finger in my direction and hisses, "He told me that after Ben left you, he was in the wrong place at the wrong time. That weekend we all went to Suffolk in the hotel Amanda organised."

My legs shake as I sit down heavily on the unmade bed as she continues to fire my shame at me like bullets that definitely find their mark.

"He told me you met in the corridor while the rest of us were in the bar, and he could tell you had been crying."

I wish she would stop because as much as I wish it was lies, it's not.

"He made to comfort you and you took advantage of his kindness and kissed him."

"It wasn't…"

She holds up her hand. "I believe him, not you, because he was man enough to confess because he couldn't live with the guilt."

I can't comprehend what I'm hearing, as she continues with a snarl.

"Apparently, you asked him to help you into your room because your fingers were shaking too much to open the door and, like a fool, he followed you inside where you proceeded to throw yourself at him. He told me he relented in a moment of weakness and one thing led to another and he ended up in your bed."

I cover my burning face with my fingers as she relays an event that happened so very differently, but happened all the same to my eternal shame.

"So, you see, Samantha, I've known all the time about your blatant attempt at taking what was mine and didn't consider my feelings once. What was your plan? To lure him away from me like Ben had already been by a younger woman. To replace your own errant husband with mine and leave me and the boys to cope alone while you took what was ours?"

"It wasn't like that." I sob, the tears trickling through the cracks in my fingers and spilling down my face.

"It was exactly like that and anything you tell me will be lies."

I am destroyed because one thing cannot be ignored. I did

have sex with her husband, and I never once considered my friend.

"I'm sorry." My voice shakes as I attempt to apologise for something that should never have happened, and I hate myself for ever allowing it to in the first place. I detest myself for not going to her, but in truth I was scared. Sonia has always intimidated me, and I've never felt comfortable around her, and now I must deal with my shame in the most unexpected of places.

Sonia sighs heavily and sits beside me on the bed, her arm reaching out and draping across my shoulders.

"It's fine. I guess." She says gently.

"I was in two minds whether to bring it up or not, but one thing I learned after Daniel's latest bombshell is that problems are best dealt with in the open. It got me thinking, and this has been an elephant in our room for too long now."

She squeezes me reassuringly. "I'm sorry to burst in here and confront you. Especially after the lovely few days we had until, well, until this morning and when I was alone with my thoughts, I concluded this was the perfect time to lay all our demons to rest."

I peer through my fingers at her surprisingly gentle face and say with a catch to my voice, "I thought you'd be angry."

"I am." She sighs heavily. "I was livid in fact, and yet I've had time to cool down and look on it more rationally. It happened when you were hurting. Grieving for something you lost, and it must have been a blow to your pride to lose your husband to a much younger, more attractive woman."

I physically wince as her words cause irreparable damage to my self-esteem, and she sighs loudly. "Don't get me wrong, it hurts. More than any other time because you are my friend Samantha. We've been through so much together, and I never really expected you to sink so low."

Every well-aimed word finds its mark and wounds me, causing me to feel like the worst person in the world. Then she offers the smallest smile and whispers, "I forgive you, Samantha. I value our friendship more than something that happened in the past when you were at your lowest point. I can move on from that. Can you?"

I nod, because she could ask me for a kidney right now and I would gladly oblige and as I smile through my tears, I congratulate myself on having a friend like Sonia who as it turns out, is bigger than all of us put together.

There has been countless times since it happened that I hated myself with a passion. Facing her would stir up the most excruciating sense of shame and self-loathing. I always wondered if this conversation would ever happen and dreaded it ever becoming a reality. However, now it's out in the open, I am free for once in my life. I can move on, knowing there are no longer any skeletons in my closet. I can begin my new life knowing I have settled the account on my old one.

With a surge of love, I reach for my friend's hand and whisper, "Thank you. I don't deserve a friend like you and if it's worth anything at all, I am so sorry, Sonia. I never meant for it to happen; I promise you that, but I can assure you it only happened once."

I add a full stop to my sentence because the last thing I'm about to admit is that Daniel was incapable of taking no for an answer. I don't reveal the barrage of texts I received and emails and unanswered calls that he plagued me with for months afterwards. There were the times he turned up at my door when it was dark and pleaded with me to let him inside to 'talk'. I knew what he wanted. Me as it happens and there are texts to prove it.

However, they can stay where they are because Sonia doesn't need to know that about her husband. It's obvious they've worked through their troubles and if she wants to believe he is the man he portrays, then that's up to them. I have a friendship to rebuild, and the subject is closed. On my part, anyway.

Sonia stands and reaches for my hand and says with a deep sigh. "We should go. The others will be waiting."

I scramble after her and as I close the door to my home from home for the past two days, I know I will be back. This is my home now and it's up to me to make it happen.

23

SAMANTHA

It's as if the fresh air has blown the clouds away and I experience a strange lightness inside that hasn't been there for some time. If anything, the guilt hasn't gone away, but the fear has. Fear of my dirty little secret coming out in the open and making my friends turn against me. None of that matters because the most important person knows, and I have nothing else to fear.

The fact she got the story wrong doesn't mean a thing. Both Daniel and I know what really happened. How he... well, some things are better left in the past and I'm not about to resurrect them. So, I close the door on my room and shut my past in with it and walk away a new woman.

It's funny how things turn out unplanned and unprepared, but now it has, I enjoy a sense of freedom I wasn't expecting.

We head downstairs in an easy silence. All the words have been said and they have no place here now. Whatever happens in our future, Sonia and I will be stronger for this. The fact I didn't correct Daniel's story is of no consequence. I buried that episode a long time ago and wrapped it up along with the pain and humiliation of my marriage breakdown and filed it away as a bad memory that had no place in my future.

Subsequently, I worked harder and devoted my time to my business and now I'm able to move everything here to Dubai.

The others are waiting for us in reception, and Ginny says ruefully.

"Well, that was short, but definitely sweet. I'll never forget this trip."

I note her holding the Chanel handbag with obvious pride and smile. "You are taking away some valuable mementoes from this trip."

She nods with a smug smile.

"Yes, it's strange how life works out, isn't it? I came here single and searching for something new and I found it in the most unexpected way."

Catherine nods. "None of us will forget this trip in a hurry. I just wish it was longer because what's waiting at home is a building storm."

I notice her anxious expression and turn my attention to the woman who stabbed our bubble with the sharpest blade, and Sonia sighs heavily. "It will all be fine. Daniel and Jasper will sort it out and it may take a little longer than we would like, but they'll get our money back somehow."

"Jasper?" Amanda stares at her with a blank expression. "What has Jasper got to do with it?"

If anything, I detect animosity between them, which doesn't go unnoticed by Catherine, who shares a concerned look my way.

"Well, obviously, he will help. It's what friends do."

Sonia says somewhat pointedly, and I'm surprised when Amanda merely nods before glancing down to the ground.

As we approach the desk, I'm not sure if it's in my imagination but there's tension in the air and as the receptionist prepares our bill, Sonia gathers us around and whispers, "Amanda has lost her purse and won't be able to pay her share."

She appears angry about that for some reason, and I say with sympathy, "That's terrible. Do you think it was stolen?"

Sonia interrupts, "Of course it wasn't stolen. This is Dubai. There is no crime."

Catherine shrugs. "Where money is concerned, there is always crime. It's a possibility."

The receptionist slips the bill towards us, and a strange atmosphere settles around us like an unwelcome guest at Sonia's leaving party.

She takes the bill and I swear winces a little as she fumbles in her purse and hands over her card. It's all a little strange, but I push it aside and reach for my own credit card to settle my part of the bill, although I doubt there is anything more than just a few drinks from beside the pool and the evening bar. Amanda said we could reimburse her for our share of the accommodation when her credit card bill comes through.

I don't pay much attention until the receptionist says politely, "I'm sorry madam, the card has been declined. Do you have another one?"

We all glance up at the same time and stare at Sonia with a mixture of disbelief and sympathy and she says loudly, "It must be a mistake. Is your machine faulty perhaps?"

The receptionist shakes her head. "No. Perhaps we could try another card."

Amanda's expression strikes me as odd because it's almost as if she is taking great pleasure from the situation and, as she catches my eye, she smiles and says with a slight shake of her head. "I'm so sorry. If only I hadn't lost my purse, this wouldn't be happening."

Sonia is flushed and appears lost for words and Ginny says sympathetically, "I'm no help, I'm afraid. My credit card stays at home because I carry a pre-paid one which I only loaded with enough money for myself."

Catherine nods. "Same. Connor says he doesn't trust me with an actual credit limit and loaded up my own pre-paid one with the bare minimum."

Of everything I've heard today, that shocks me the most as I stare at my friend in surprise. Since when did Catherine allow her husband to control her spending? I always thought they were loaded, and money was never a problem. Why would he be so controlling? It doesn't make sense?

The desolation on Sonia's face makes up my mind in an instant and I step forward, waving my own card at the receptionist.

"Add that one to mine." I say with a reassuring smile. "You can pay me back when we get home. I'm sure it's all a technical issue, anyway."

If anything, Amanda appears annoyed but disguises it quickly and smiles her thanks as Sonia says loudly, "Thanks

Samantha, at least I can count on one of my friends in a moment of crisis."

Her words raise a few brows and yet I bask in them. Yes, this is the least I owe Sonia after her gracious acceptance of what happened and then, as I glance at the itemised bill, I feel my legs shake.

Ten thousand pounds. I don't believe it. Who spends ten thousand pounds in a few days?

The words swim before my disbelieving eyes as I register the cost of the suite, the spa treatments, meals and the drinks bill. Bottles of prosecco rival the finest champagne in price. Cocktails, signature coffees and meals in the a la carte restaurant are many and visits to the hotel patisserie and gifts from the shop add up to an amount that staggers me.

As my card sags under the burden of my guilt, I paste a brave smile on my face as Sonia slaps me on the back. "Thank you, Samantha. You're a true friend. As soon as we get home, Amanda will ping the money across if you text her your bank details."

I stare at Amanda in shock and note the narrowing of her eyes and the tightening of her lips as she glares at Sonia with an animosity I've never seen before. Then she says firmly, "I will reimburse you for my share. Of course I will, and Sonia will reimburse you for hers."

I note the sharp look Sonia directs her way and, if anything, she appears a little shocked. "But we agreed."

"What did we agree, Sonia?"

Amanda stares at her with a blank expression, causing Sonia to stumble over her words. "It's our arrangement and always has been."

Amanda shrugs. "We don't have an arrangement, Sonia. Now if I'm not mistaken, the minibus is waiting, and we have a flight to catch. Perhaps we should discuss this later."

She turns away, effectively cutting Sonia off, and Catherine catches my eye and smiles weakly.

I stare after my departing friends and wonder just what I've missed because something appears to have gone very wrong between two best friends who grew up together.

24

GINNY

I'm not sure what I missed, but something has happened. I've been so wrapped up in my own misery, I never saw this coming. As soon as Sonia told me the devastating news, my mind has been scrambled and as I sit beside Catherine on the bus, I lower my voice to a harsh whisper.

"How are you bearing up? That was some bombshell Sonia threw at us this morning."

Catherine nods and says with a deep sigh. "I'm trying not to think about it. Connor will be unbearable and, quite frankly, the thought of going home to face him is not a pleasant one. What about you, though?

From the sound of it, this affects you more than any of us?"

A sharp pain hits me as I face my ruin and I say sharply, "I feel like a fool."

"Why?" Catherine's face is a picture of concern and I sigh. "I never sought advice. I went ahead and re-mortgaged my house because I trusted Daniel. Who does that?"

"He can be very persuasive." Catherine says thoughtfully and I shrug dejectedly. "Even so, I should have investigated it a bit more and asked for Jasper's advice, perhaps."

"Do you think they invested?" Catherine says with a sly look in our fortunate friend's direction.

"I don't know. Probably not if it was a bad investment. Men like Jasper don't rise to the top if they make mistakes. I'm guessing he makes very few of them due to the wealth they enjoy."

"I suppose." Catherine hesitates before saying with a frown. "I'm dreading going home."

"Connor?" From the expression on her face, I've hit the mark, and she appears so worried it chases my own demons away for a moment.

"Why?"

I'm concerned for my friend because I never once considered she was anything but happy, however, at the mention of the pre-paid card and her reluctance to head home, tells me she's been suffering in full view, and we were all blind to it.

"It's well..." The desperation on her face makes my blood run cold and I watch a lone tear form in the corner of her eye that she blinks furiously away.

"I don't love him anymore."

I just stare as she appears amazed at the sound of her own words and then, feeling a little braver, says in a whisper. "I'm not sure I ever did."

The bus stops at some traffic lights and the noise of the engine is muted for a moment, giving us time to digest what she said.

I note the conversation is limited around us as Sonia sits beside Samantha, leaving Amanda to sit on her own in front. Each one of them appears lost in contemplation and, as the engine starts again, I whisper, "Do you want to talk about it?"

She nods, which is another surprise because in all the years I've known her, Catherine has maintained a polite silence when it comes to her own thoughts and feelings.

"Do you mind, but not here?"

"On the flight, perhaps?" I ask and she nods, throwing me a grateful smile. "I would like that."

"What about Samantha? Do you mind if she knows?"

"Not really. It may be the perfect time to scrape a whole load of shit off my chest."

The fact she swore makes me raise my eyes because when did Catherine ever swear? I didn't think she even knew the words because she certainly never uses them.

For some reason it makes me laugh and her giggle is a welcome distraction from the gloom we have settled under and as we head through the streets of Dubai, we could be back on that coach taking us on a school trip all those years ago back at Summerhouse High .

———

When we reach Dubai airport, we join the line to check in. Three of us, anyway. Sonia and Amanda head to the empty Club World check in and once again I stare enviously at my entitled friend.

"One day." I murmur almost to myself although that day appears to have passed already. I'll be lucky to travel at all because I must face the fact that when I get home, I may not have a penny to my name.

As Sonia and Amanda head through fast-track security and onward to their complimentary lounge, the rest of us stand with the masses and wait our turn, due to the fact we never had the money to upgrade our lives.

Catherine is quiet beside me and appears engrossed in her phone, and I'm surprised to see the delight in her eyes and the small smile on her lips as she bashes out a text. I doubt it's her husband bringing happiness to her desperate situation and expect it's from her daughter Sally. The apple of her eye and her best friend, us aside.

Samantha whispers, "If we're lucky, we won't be back in England for long. Are you still up for moving here?"

"With what?" I say in despair. "I've lost everything – remember?"

Samantha brushes off my salty response and says with determination. "Then it may be the perfect time for a change."

"How?" She shrugs and, in this moment, I have a newfound respect for my usually quiet friend.

"Listen, Ginny." I'm surprised at the firmness in her tone as she faces me with a stern expression. "I lost everything once. Everything I considered worth keeping, anyway. It turns out I was wrong. Yes, I got the house but also took on the mortgage, which as it turns out, isn't far off the value of the house, anyway. I had no savings and no pension, and the only thing left was my business."

I stare at her with interest as she opens up a little more detail on her life and, to my surprise, she grins.

"I'm going to rent out my house to pay the mortgage and I don't see why you can't do the same. You see, unlike you, I was nowhere near paying it off and so I have no choice, really.

Keep my asset but realise its potential and relocate my business to a tax-free haven. I will rent an apartment there and leave my own house with a letting agent and walk away. If it doesn't work out in Dubai, I have a home to come back to and my business can operate anywhere."

Her eyes sparkle as she says in a low, excited whisper, "You could do the same. Cut your losses and move with me. Set up a real estate business in Dubai, or work for one already established. They would bite your hand off with your experience and I'm not even kidding. I have been investigating how to make it happen and it's a strong possibility."

She reaches out and touches my arm in a gentle show of support.

"What happened sucks. I know that, but it could also be the catalyst for change. You can pay off the debt with the rental money and still keep your asset. You never know, Jasper may still save the day and you'll be back to square one again. Think about it, please. I'd love to go on this adventure with you."

The conversation is cut short as we reach the front of the line, and it reminds me of a saying I always lived by.

If you want to be successful, you must join the line because one day you will reach the front of it.

It's true, at least I always hoped it was and now Samantha is shining a torch on the dark tunnel I just found myself in. Of course, she's right. There is always a way out and it just requires a little light on the situation to reveal the exit. Far from my world ending, my new one is just beginning and so as we approach the desk, it's with a bright smile firmly plastered on my face.

25
GINNY

As soon as we hit duty free, I am reminded once again of how little money I have. Everything is so expensive, and I can't even afford a snack in the restaurant. I am officially broken because even though I earn a good wage from my business, it all gets swallowed up in the current cost-of-living crisis. I used the last of my meagre savings to pay for this trip, once again reminding me how different my life is from my friends, except for Samantha, I suppose. Then again, she did have a husband once, and they shared an income and decisions, and it must have felt good. I never have. I've always been alone and everything I have I've worked damned hard for, which makes this current situation even more difficult to deal with.

The fact I've used men as entertainment all my life is coming back to bite me hard because I have nobody to confide in except for my friends, which shows how sad my life really is.

I've always tried not to let it get to me when I've spent Christmas and Easter watching television rather than with family. I occasionally enjoyed time with a current boyfriend, but I get bored easily and when they aren't as motivated as me, I lose interest pretty damned quickly.

My thoughts turn to Omar, and I wonder if it will be different with him. Is a man like that just what I need?

No commitment but a whole load of fun when our paths cross. A loner like me who places work in front of anything else. But for what? I thought I was doing well and lost everything in a heartbeat and now all that's left is the realisation I had nothing of value at all. I never have because surely having a family is the utmost wealth a person can enjoy and I kind of missed the lesson on that somewhere along the way in my pursuit of wealth and privilege.

I glance down at my designer handbag which, for some reason, leaves me cold. I could have purchased a car with the money Omar paid for this, which disgusts me a little. A handbag shouldn't cost so much and if it does, the person buying it should know better. Suddenly, it's a symbol of everything that's wrong with my life and it sickens me. *I* sicken me and so I stop for a moment and consider where I go from here.

"Is everything okay?" A concerned voice edges into my thoughts, and I glance at Catherine with a nod.

"I think so." I smile and it's as if a weight has lifted as I glance back at the inanimate object that has pivoted me onto a different path.

"I'm sure everything will be just fine, actually."

I smile, noting her amazed expression, which makes me grin.

"Come, let's grab a coffee in Starbucks. It turns out that's all I really need right now."

Catherine raises her eyes and follows me, and Samantha says quickly, "I'll just head into duty free and see if I can pick up some perfume for my mum. It's Mother's Day soon and I don't want to forget to buy her anything."

As she heads off, I think about my own mother who lives in Wales now and make a pledge to go and visit her at the first available opportunity because suddenly money is no longer as important to me as people, and I like how that makes me feel.

As we settle down with a hot steaming coffee, I notice that Catherine is glued to her phone again and say casually, "Somebody is popular."

She blushes slightly, which surprises me, because if that's not a sign of a guilty conscience, I don't know what is.

I stare at her pointedly and she places it inside her bag and grabs her coffee.

"Oh, it's nothing."

"You seriously expect me to believe that?"

I shake my head and am surprised when she leans forward and says in a whisper, "Listen, don't say a thing, but if anyone understands what I'm about to say, it's probably you."

"Go on." Now I'm intrigued, and she giggles, reverting to the school kid she was over thirty years ago and she says with a flush to her cheek, "I joined a dating app."

For a moment, I wonder if I'm in a parallel universe and say guardedly, "Because…"

She shrugs and her eyes flash as she says roughly, "Because my husband's an arsehole who controls my life so much, I've fallen out of love with him."

I say nothing because what the hell is going on right now? It's as if we've stumbled into another dimension where everything turns the other way around.

She sighs and appears distracted as she sips her coffee before saying sadly, "I can't remember when it started, really. I certainly never noticed it happening, but every aspect of my life became planned by him."

She shakes her head in disgust and I'm not sure if it's aimed at him, or her as she says wearily, "My entire life revolves around what Connor wants. How I bring up our daughter, how I dress and how he wants the house. I have no opinion and if I offer one, I'm shot down and made out to be a fool."

"The bastard." I throw out through gritted teeth, and she nods. "He is. Perhaps it was the love dust he threw in my eyes that blinded me to his faults, or it could be the lifestyle I became accustomed to. He was successful, *is successful* and reminded me of that every opportunity he got. I was the one who ran to keep up with him and as the main bread winner he controlled the finances and when I say control, I mean he grabbed them in an iron fist."

"I never knew." I stare at her sadly because how did I not notice that my friend was unhappy?

"As I said, even I didn't see it coming, and it's only lately I've opened my eyes a little. Perhaps because he's been especially bad lately and now I know why."

"The consortium?"

She nods. "It must be. He took our life savings and

ploughed them into an investment without the courtesy of even telling me, and I wonder if he ever will."

"What, are you saying he will attempt to hide this from you?"

"Probably. He never discusses business with me at all and part of me is wondering if we are as well off as I thought we were."

"What makes you say that?"

"Because he keeps such a close grip on money, I suppose. It's been getting worse, not better and even Sally has been refused school trips and extra-curricular activities that he considers a waste of time and money."

"Is that why you're interested in internet dating? To find someone else?"

As I say the words, I don't really believe them myself and hate that she winces and shakes her head.

"I guess it's because I'm lonely."

She appears so pitiful, but I understand a lot about that so I smile reassuringly. "I get that."

"It's just a little fun, really. I wouldn't dare do it at home and while I was here, I thought I'd learn what all the fuss is about and as soon as we get home, I'll delete the app. I just wanted to see if anyone still found me attractive. I wouldn't actually meet anyone. It was just an experiment to make me feel good about myself."

"Did it work?" I smile as she grins.

"Yes. I've had messages from five men and every one of them has something positive about them. It's been fun to be flirty again, but that's all it will be. A bit of fun for a few days, nothing more."

"Are you sure about that?"

I'm not convinced, and she shrugs. "It has to be. If Connor ever found out, my life wouldn't be worth living."

"Have you ever considered leaving him?"

"NO!" Her eyes are wide as she barks out the word, more in shock than anything else.

"Why not?" I shrug. "It happens."

"To other people."

She shakes her head sadly. "But not me. I don't cheat despite what I've done, and marriage is for life, for me, anyway."

"So, you would remain miserable to satisfy your principles?"

"Yes." She sighs heavily. "I never pretended to be anything but a fool, Ginny. I know how it sounds and how it appears but I couldn't put Sally through the mess it would create. I am not strong enough to leave him. He would carve me up for breakfast, lunch and dinner and I'd end up with nothing."

"Except your happiness." I remind her and she groans.

"I wouldn't be happy. Connor would make sure of it. I'm not strong enough, so I'll take my kicks while I can get them and wait and discover what fate has in store for me."

I'm not sure if I respect her, or pity her right now because she is both strong and weak at the same time, and I lean back and say firmly, "There is only one guarantee in life, Catherine. You are born alone, and you will die alone. People may come and go, but the one person you can't shake is yourself. Do what's right for you and then those around you will be happy. Maybe not at first, but you can't live your life for them. Trust me on this. I've made it my mantra, which is probably why I'm still on my own."

She stares at me and then we both burst out laughing as she chuckles, "You are a misguided example, Ginny. You stumble through life intent on perfection, and have probably found it doesn't exist. Sometimes you must compromise and accept that not everything in life is available."

"You're probably right. It's not as if I've made great decisions myself really, but I've had fun along the way I suppose."

She nods. "You know, I've always envied you."

"Really?" I'm amazed because surely, it's the other way around.

"Yes. You've made your way alone and have a successful career and until earlier, had almost paid off your house. You live your life with no inhibitions and don't care what anyone else thinks as demonstrated by your fling with the gorgeous Omar. Nobody to judge you and tell you what to do. You are a free spirit and who wouldn't be jealous of that?"

"Only someone who has no freedom, I guess."

I stare at her with a hard expression. "Don't waste time on saving something that was lost years ago. Move on and you won't be alone. Your friends are with you every step of the way and if you need to get away, a fresh start even, come to Dubai with Samantha and me."

"So, you're going ahead with it?"

I nod with a determination I never had until this conversation.

"Samantha reminded me there are always options. I just need to figure out the best one for me and then, yes, I think it will lead me back here. You may loan your mind to someone else for a bit, but it's time to wrench it back and make your own decision. The fact you even downloaded that app tells me you're ready, so stand tall and walk back into your home as the strong women you are deep down. What's there to lose, anyway?"

As the silence falls between us while we contemplate new beginnings, it's as if anything is possible right now. Change is beckoning, and we are all facing a crossroads in our lives. I'm excited to head down a different path and I have a feeling I won't be walking on it alone.

26

AMANDA

Sonia is angry. I'm getting the silent treatment and I couldn't care less.

She deserves to stew in her own mess, and I'm fed up with always being the one to dig her out of the holes she has made a career of falling into.

We take our seats in the airport lounge and I order a salad and a glass of champagne. Sonia places her own order and I resign myself to catching up with the book on my kindle for the rest of the flight.

As I fire it up, Sonia says with a sigh, "This is a mess."

"It is." I glance down at the screen and she says angrily,

"Daniel is such an idiot. I've lost count of the times he's let me down."

"What happened?"

I rest my kindle on my lap and stare at her with concern because despite everything I am concerned for her and her sons. Daniel is like a lit firework hurled into a crowd because he is uncontrollable and liable to do a lot of damage and always has been. It's why he's lost more jobs than anyone I have ever met, and I'm still astounded that he continues to be employed in the financial sector at all. Jasper has told me countless times he has a terrible reputation and yet he always manages to pull it out of the bag when he needs to, which is why Sonia's comment about Jasper helping him infuriated me.

Sonia surprises me by slumping back in her seat and running her fingers through her usually perfectly coffered hair.

"I begged him not to include my friends in his schemes, but he was adamant they would profit from it."

"Why didn't you warn them?" I'm curious about that, and she shrugs. "Why would I? How could I admit my husband is a jackass and couldn't make it even if he had a time machine and flew back in time and found out the lottery numbers? He's an idiot and always has been."

This is new and I wonder when Sonia stopped defending her husband and I say gently, "So what are you saying?"

"I don't know." She sighs.

"The thing is, Amanda." She stops and appears to be struggling with something and then sighs. "I have always wanted to be you."

"Me?" I'm shocked and she nods, studying her fingernails as if the answers lie there. "When I introduced you to Jasper, I never imagined he would become so successful."

"Would that have changed anything?" I'm confused, and she forces out an insincere laugh. "Of course not. It's just, well, I was always the one with the successful boyfriend. The man everyone expected to succeed, and he did at first."

"That's not important." I shake my head. "You fell in love. Surely that was the most important thing."

"Love." Sonia almost spits the word. "Love never came into it. You see, I knew from a very young age I wanted to be rich. To be one of those Range Rover mums without a care in the world. Dropping her kids off to school before spending the day shopping or at the country club. That was going to be my life and I made calculating decisions based on it."

I am silent because I have no words. It's certainly not something I ever knew about. She huffs. "I should have married Jasper."

"Was it ever an option?" I say with controlled rage, and she shrugs. "Probably not. I mean, we only met him through Daniel's work, so he had his uses. No, before I introduced him to you, I should have realised he was a better bet and kept him for myself."

"I doubt that would have happened." I say sharply, because can this woman sink any lower?

She shrugs. "Maybe not, but you did okay out of it. You got the man who is good at his job. The perfect home, holidays, luxuries and children who want for nothing and it was all handed to you on a plate."

I am spared from answering as our food is delivered and as her words form a solid wall between our friendship, I decide to say nothing at all. Sonia's friendship, as it turns out, is not as described in the dictionary and I doubt she has ever understood the meaning of the word.

As she drinks her champagne, I mull over her words and think back to a time when things were different. We were friends through our mothers and were forced together because of it. Playdays, sleepovers and family parties. I went to a different school, but we were friends outside. However, I am struggling to remember a time when I didn't live in her shadow. I suppose I was always grateful that such a popular girl would want to be friends with me. Nobody at my own school wanted to, and I soon became an honorary member of the Summerhouse girls, and I was eternally grateful for that.

The trouble is, when do you stop being grateful? When are you accepted as one of them in your own right and not just because of who introduced you into the group? I've always felt a little excluded. Not intentionally, but they would talk of things that happened at school that I knew nothing about. It's always been them with me running behind, desperate to fit in and so I keep it together and drain my glass of champagne, contemplating the move I am resigned to making when I get home.

Luckily, the flight is on time, and we board and head to our seats that thankfully provide privacy. I won't need to make conversation with my dubious friend and can wrap myself in a bubble for the remainder of the flight and plan my next course of action.

Whatever Daniel has done will not be unravelled by my husband, and if I have my way, nothing will ever be the same again.

I'm a little nervous as I contemplate the idea that has been brewing for months now. Can I really pull it off or will it crash and burn? I am so nervous and wonder what Jasper will think when I ask for his help. Our relationship isn't as perfect as everyone seems to think because it's difficult admitting that your husband is a virtual stranger and always has been.

Sonia said I was the lucky one – I disagree. Wealth has come at a price and loneliness is a huge price to pay. I can't even remember the last time we had a date night, or a trip away together without the kids. When did he last tell me he loved me and compliment me on my appearance? When I change something in the house, he doesn't even notice until I point it out and when he heads home, he merely retreats to his study to work on his private investments.

No. I don't consider myself the lucky one at all. That description belongs to a different person entirely. A woman I admire and strive to emanate because who on this earth wouldn't want to be her, anyway?

Ginny is the person I admire most in the world and I have always hung onto every word she said and waited to hear the latest instalment of her life story with bated breath. Who wouldn't want to be a strong independent woman and the fact Sonia has stolen her money is not sitting well with me?

Then there's Catherine and Connor. If it just concerned him, I wouldn't care less, but Catherine doesn't deserve to lose everything. She is kind, thoughtful and loyal and of all my friends, she is the one I am most comfortable with. She has an inner kindness that radiates positivity, something I could gorge on right now. The fact Samantha paid our hotel bill was a plot twist I never saw coming and makes me more determined than ever. Then there's me. The gullible fool who has made a career as a doormat. Finally, realising that best friend is just another word for betrayal.

Yes, I have six hours to plan my revenge and by the end of it, thirty years of trying will count for thirty years of lying because it's doubtful I ever had friends, anyway.

27
AMANDA

It's good to be home. Despite everything that happened, home has always been my sanctuary.

As I open the door, the only person waiting to greet me is my mother and seeing her warm, friendly face causes me to drop my bag and run into her open arms.

As her arms fold around me, it's so good to be held by someone who has always had my best interests at heart and I whisper, "Thanks mum."

She pulls back and smiles, a hint of concern in her eyes that I eradicate with a brave smile.

"So, how has it been? Did they all behave themselves?"

"I hardly saw them, if I'm honest." She grumbles, rolling her eyes.

"Now I know what the saying alone in a crowd means. No wonder you keep yourself so busy, darling. A person could go mad around here, stuck in this large space with only the echoes of their thoughts to keep them company."

"It's not so bad." This time I roll my eyes and she grins.

"Possibly not, but it concerns me a little."

"It's fine. I'm used to it and won't be for much longer anyway."

"Why not?"

"Because Jasper told me he would retire when he reached fifty-five and as it happens, that's only next year."

Mum grins and her eye roll is way over-exaggerated. "And pigs will pilot rockets to the moon. Honestly, Amanda, that man invented the term workaholic."

I grin because she's not wrong and as I make us both a coffee, I experience a pang of fondness for my husband. The fact he works so hard has become part of him and it's difficult to imagine life being any different. However, it's always been that way and I've grown accustomed to it. All the time the children were young and dependent on me, my days were full, and I was needed. Now, not so much, which is probably why I'm struggling a little, and I suppose it's not Jasper's fault.

Mum stays to hear about my trip and I gloss over most of what happened and only when I wave her off do I retrieve my own case and haul it to my dressing room.

As I unzip the case, a small smile escapes when I retrieve my purse from the zipped compartment and experience a twinge of satisfaction that for once I made life a little difficult for my friend.

It's just unfortunate she pulled the rabbit out of the hat

and Samantha paid because I was looking forward to watching her squirm while facing up to her own overindulgence.

"Hey."

I jump out of my skin as a familiar voice strikes me like a dart to my heart and I turn, not really expecting anyone to be there. However, as I turn, it's to witness a miracle because leaning against the door looking so incredibly gorgeous is the man who likes to work too hard.

"Jasper." I whisper in disbelief and his low chuckle makes me smile as he crosses the room and takes me in his arms, pulling me close against his warm muscular chest and holding the back of my head in a rare show of affection.

"I missed you." He says huskily and I must be dreaming because this has never happened before and then he whispers close to my ear, "I'm sorry, Amanda."

Now I'm panicking because what has he done to be sorry about? Is it another woman? Has he made a shaky investment that crashed, causing us to lose everything? Was he involved in the consortium or, God forbid, did he have an affair?

I'm speechless as he whispers, "I've been the worst husband in the world, and I apologise for that."

"What's brought this on?" I find my voice and pulling back, peer anxiously into his eyes to see the man I fell in love with staring back at me.

"They say distance makes the heart grow fonder and, well, I've been thinking a lot about us lately."

"And?" I hold my breath as he smiles. "I'm going to take early retirement and make it up to you."

My mind is scrambled because what happened while I was away and he strokes my face and whispers, "After you called, it struck me how distant we've become."

I make to speak, but he holds up his hand and says with a

sigh. "I blame myself. I've always put work first which made me think about the years I've lost out on. The kids' school days, weekends as a family and just being with you."

"What's brought this on?"

I'm ecstatic but concerned, and he shrugs. "I was listening to a song in the car on the way home that struck me deep. The one where a man has no time for his son growing up and when he does have that time, his son has moved on and become just like him. I am that father, Amanda, and I am that husband and I'm terrified that when I'm ready, nobody will be waiting."

My heart actually melts when I note the concern on his face, and he says with a smile. "We have enough money now. The house is paid off, our pensions are full, and our investments will mean we never have to dip into it. How much money can a person ever earn to make them truly happy? When is it enough before you start reaping the benefits of that? So, I've handed in my resignation, and I leave in three months. Plan a holiday, in fact, plan the rest of our lives because the most important thing in mine and always has been, is you."

It's as if every doubt, every concern, and every bit of pain falls away at his words and the future is bright. Somehow, I've got my husband back and no amount of money in the world can pay for that.

I can't ever remember a time when I spent the afternoon in bed with my husband. Even in the early days, it never happened and now, after the most surprising conversation of my life, we lie entwined in each other's arms, and I really believe I am the lucky one and have it all.

We talk about the future and things we want to do, and I am so happy I could burst. I have no worries about the future now and who I walk into it with. Jasper has come back to me, which makes me invincible.

Just before the kids are due home, I make my husband a coffee in our state-of-the-art kitchen that was purchased only last year, and we talk about my trip.

I fill him in, and he shakes his head. "You're better off without Sonia."

"I know." I sit beside him at the breakfast bar and say with a deep sigh. "Maybe it's time to call in the favour."

"What do you mean?"

I think carefully before I answer because once this starts, I won't be able to change it back and I hesitate before saying, "You know how our friendship worked. Sonia invited me and I paid for everything."

Jasper shrugs. "I thought you were happy about that."

"Why would I be?" I say through gritted teeth.

"At first it was to help her out. The odd meal because Daniel had a bad month. A tab settled on her birthday by way of a gift. A helping hand because she left her purse at home and clothes for the kids because their investments were tied up."

Jasper nods. "I'll admit it's unusual, but we have the money and it's good to help friends."

"Who need it to eat. Not to book expensive holidays with our money and go off on a jolly. Not to invite every friend they have to a birthday bash courtesy of yours truly. Not to keep up appearances on their behalf just to disguise they aren't doing as well as everyone thought they were. That's not friendship, Jasper, that's desperation."

He nods thoughtfully. "So don't do it anymore."

"I've already made that decision. In fact..."

I tell him what happened in Dubai, and he laughs out loud. "I would have loved to see the look on her face when she had to pay for everything."

"It was interesting, but Samantha has stepped into my shoes and won't ever receive Sonia's share of the debt if I know my dubious best friend."

"So, pay it. Samantha shouldn't be out of pocket."

"She won't be."

Jasper leans back and grins.

"I recognise that look. What are you plotting now?"

"Revenge, dear husband. Basic primal revenge because she has stepped on the last shred of kindness I had left in me."

He stares at me with interest, and I tap my fingers on the counter and say casually. "But I need your help."

28

CATHERINE

My heart is heavy when I head inside the huge wooden front door. My fingers actually shake as I wrestle with the key in the lock, and I half expect to see Connor waiting for me with a furious expression and knowledge of my dating app.

I'm not cut out for espionage, and yet something prevented me from deleting the app in the cab on the way home from the station.

I just couldn't do it. Instead, I changed the password on my phone, intent on keeping my delicious secret for a few days longer just to make my homecoming bearable.

As the walls close around me, I hate how it makes me feel. Home should be where the heart is, not where the hate is.

At least I have Sally, but she is away on a school trip and won't be home until tomorrow. Luckily, my parents paid for it for her birthday because she had the sense to mention it to them before she asked us.

I hate knowing our own daughter has felt the new restrictions and the tense atmosphere in this house has extinguished a little of the light from her eyes.

It was such a gradual process I don't think either of us realised it was happening until we could no longer ignore it. This is not a happy home anymore, and I am struggling to remember when it was.

As I unpack and place my clothes in the laundry basket, I wonder when I will need them again. If Connor has lost everything, it's doubtful trips away will be on the agenda.

With a sigh, I head to our room and stare around at a space devoid of anything but pain because sleeping beside my husband is always done with bated breath until he falls asleep, signalling I am no longer required for the night. Not that we have sex often. Rarely, in fact, and usually only when he has a little too much to drink. Even then it's cold, emotionless, and slightly aggressive and I can't remember when it's ever been anything else.

I note the unmade bed and the anger bubbles up inside me because he couldn't even be bothered to pull the covers across.

As I lift the duvet to make the bed, my heart stops beating when I notice an object that isn't mine.

My fingers shake as I lift a pair of knickers that are definitely against the trade descriptions act because the scrap of fabric in my hand would barely cover one half of my own backside.

With a feeling of nausea, I drop them to the ground and sink onto the side of the bed, my eyes glued to the incriminating evidence. As I try to make sense of it all, the most noteworthy thing is why I'm not sobbing right now.

In fact, I'm more confused knowing that anyone else would find Connor attractive because he let himself go years ago. In fact, his beer belly and thinning hair reveal the middle-aged man he became when I wasn't looking. It almost amuses me to think of his photograph on my dating app because it's certainly not appealing and yet as I see the evidence with my own eyes, it's obvious somebody disagrees with that.

I'm not sure what to do because this changes everything and yet changes nothing too. I have fallen out of love with my husband and obviously it's right back at me because as soon as my back was turned, he moved another woman into our bed.

I wondered why he agreed for me to go on this trip and now I know why. He was auditioning for my replacement, at least I hope he was because this has made my decision much easier.

If anything, I have a lightness in spirit that wasn't here when I left and with a wry grin I reach for my phone and scroll to the message from Jack Bennett.

I tap out a response.

CATHY

> Sorry for the delay. I've been on a long-haul flight. Yes, I would love to meet up. Do you have somewhere in mind?

As I press send, it's in the knowledge I am doing the right thing. If Ginny can put herself first, so can I.

Two hours later, my heart lurches when the front door slams and my errant husband heads into the kitchen with a short, "Oh, you're back then."

"Obviously." I don't even try to disguise the irritation in my voice, and he glances up and says, "You're in a bad mood. You know, that menopause you're going through is beginning to irritate the hell out of me."

I never knew that blood could actually boil. Either it's through anger or that menopause he refers to, but I imagine it's the former and I suppose it's the last freaking straw.

"I want a divorce."

The words surprise me more than him as he stares at me in shock.

"What did you say?" He says in disbelief, and I start laughing slightly hysterically.

"What's the matter with you? Are you drunk? Under the influence of alcohol, or drugs, even?" He looks so surprised it makes me giggle and I say in a carefree voice, "None of the above. I've just woken up to a better future without you in it."

He drops his briefcase and slumps down on the chair at the table and, to my surprise, says in a trembling voice, "Why?"

I can't believe he's even asking me this because surely, he must realise we aren't working anymore.

I take a seat opposite him and say gently, "Be truthful, Connor. This isn't working."

"What isn't?" He appears genuinely confused and I shrug. "Our marriage. For years now, you've treated me like one of your employees. I'm not even allowed my own mind anymore, and you cut me down, whatever I say."

"No, I don't."

He fixes me with a hard glare. "You say I've changed. What about you?"

"What about me?"

I can't wait to hear what he's on about, and he hisses. "You are permanently tired. You don't try anymore. Everything seems like a chore, and you constantly nag. You're not interested in sex and lie there like a frigid bitch every time I try to get a response out of you."

The last shred of dignity I possess explodes as I toss the thong on the table and yell, "Is that why you've been screwing another woman in our bed?"

I relish the sudden pallor of his complexion as he stares at the offending article that has revealed his duplicity far more than any words could.

I carry on and snarl, "And when exactly were you going to tell me you gambled away our life savings on a recommendation from Daniel?"

Now he appears about to throw up and says in shock. "You know about that."

"Don't look so surprised, Connor. I've been away with his wife for the past two days and at least she had the decency to tell me. Were you ever going to, and what about that?"

I scream the last word as I point at the lace thong staring smugly up at me, causing me to burst into tears and slump back on my seat.

I'm not sure who is more shocked, me or Connor, because when do I ever cry? Never. But I can't stop now, and I place my hands over my face and cry for everything. My failed marriage and the fact I've wasted so many years on a man who didn't deserve them. For losing everything and for my daughter, who is about to learn a valuable life lesson as she deals with being the product of a broken home. More than anything though, I'm crying with relief because I've finally stood up for myself and it's been a long time coming.

I'm surprised when a gentle hand pulls me around and he wraps his arms around me.

"I'm sorry, Cathy."

I say nothing as he rocks me like a baby and says mournfully, "You're right. I've behaved abominably, and you have every right to demand a divorce."

I pull back and stare at him through sad eyes. "Thank you."

He looks confused and I sniff. "That's the first time in a very long time that you have spoken to me as if I count."

He glances down and I pull away and stare at the pair of almost knickers.

"Who is she?" I'm mildly interested, and he shrugs. "Someone I picked up off the streets, if you must know."

"A prostitute?" I'm horrified, and this time it's Connor who places his head in his hands.

"I'm sorry. It started by accident, and I became addicted."

"To what?" I'm so confused, and he says in a small voice. "Sex with prostitutes."

"Since when?" Now I'm disgusted and feel physically sick, and he says with a hint of shame, "It was the only control I had left. The business was slipping further away from me, and you weren't interested in me anymore. One night I saw a woman on the street corner, and something snapped inside me. I picked her up and she well, she performed a service on me, and I paid her. I thought that would be the end of it, but I wanted more. Last night was the first time I brought one home; I swear to you. Sally is away and so were you, and I thought it would be safer. That I wouldn't be caught."

I'm not sure what I'm feeling as I stare at the man I used to think was so strong and had it all worked out, but I'm starting to understand my life has been seen through a distorted mirror.

Everything has changed and I no longer like what I see and so I say icily, "Don't say anymore. I don't want to hear your reasons because they are just excuses. What I said before still stands. I want a divorce, Connor, and I want half of whatever is left. Sally will live with me, and you can make your own arrangements with her regarding visits. I'm done."

I stand and experience a sense of empowerment I really wasn't expecting and walk away much stronger than when I walked in. For now, we will co-exist until everything is finalised, but one thing is definite, there is no going back for me.

29

SONIA

The boys are home and glance up as I head into the living room as they slouch on the settee watching a football game.

"You're back then." Thomas shovels some crisps into his mouth and stares at me with zero interest and James says, without taking his eyes off the game. "I could murder a cup of tea."

"Not as much as I could murder you right now!" I yell and they shrug, having heard it all before.

As I head into the kitchen, I wonder what I've done to deserve two ungrateful teenagers who really should have grown out of this by now. However, rather than head for the kettle, I stop by the wine cooler and pull out a bottle of prosecco and almost tear off the cap with my teeth.

So much for going away. I was missed as much as an irritating rash and as I pour myself a glass, I prepare to discover that the game is up and life as we know it has gone forever when Daniel comes home.

I don't have to wait long either and the door slams while I am making spaghetti Bolognese for our dinner.

He saunters into the kitchen and says cheerily, "Ah, the wanderer returns. I hope you didn't bankrupt me."

"I was about to say the same to you." I point the dripping wooden spoon in his direction, and he holds up his hands. "It's all fine; we'll work it out."

"Who's we?" I slam the spoon into the pan and bash it in the sauce while wishing it was Daniel's head instead and he shrugs. "I told you. I'll ask Jasper. He'll help work it out. There must be something we can do?"

"What did Connor say when you told him?"

I'm curious, and he drops his briefcase on the table and sighs. "He was concerned, of course, but I reassured him we could pull it back."

"But you said you were going to tell him the game was over?"

A sense of dread is creeping up on me as he shrugs. "That was then. I've had a conversation with a shit hot lawyer, and he told me he'd take a look."

"A lawyer! We can't afford that. My credit card was declined."

I'm incredulous, and he shakes his head as he reaches for the gin bottle.

"A minor inconvenience that will be resolved as soon as fresh money comes through."

"What fresh money?"

"Jasper. I told you."

"You think Jasper is going to give you money?"

He turns and stares directly at me and says roughly, "Not Jasper, Amanda."

The spoon hovers in mid-air, as I say in confusion. "What's Amanda got to do with this?"

"She's your best friend and when you tell her we're desperate, she'll bail us out like she's always done."

"You want me to go begging to her?"

I'm incensed, and he nods. "Why not? It wouldn't be the first time, after all."

"No!"

My voice wobbles a little as the blood rushes to my head because the last person I want to go begging on my knees to is Amanda.

"Don't be so selfish. I'm doing everything I can to dig us out of this hole, and this is the perfect answer."

"I'm not asking her. We've, um, fallen out."

"Then apologise." He takes a long slug of gin and tonic and says with disinterest. "You'll make up, you always do, and she'll be so grateful she'll agree to anything."

"It's complicated." I have a headache coming on and he snaps, "So is life. We must call in every favour we are owed because if we go under, you can say goodbye to the comfortable life you've expected me to provide while you do absolutely nothing to contribute to it."

"What do mean I don't contribute? I'm contributing now by making you all dinner. I'm contributing when I wash your clothes and clean the house. Send your family birthday cards and arrange gifts at Christmas and birthdays."

I slam the spoon into the sauce, feeling like hurling it across the room instead and yell, "I contribute when I ferry the boys around to their clubs and feed their friends. I organise the home, so you don't have to lift a finger when you're here by arranging handy men to do the job most other husbands are keen to pitch in to. How dare you say I don't contribute because, quite frankly, my contribution is worth a lot more than yours because the only thing you contribute to my life is one big giant fucking headache."

Daniel stares at me as he would a small child throwing a tantrum and just closes the kitchen door before saying calmly. "You're jetlagged and you've been at the bottle again. Maybe now is the perfect time to discuss your drinking problem."

The fact the knife block is an arm's reach away is not a good omen for Daniel but adding murder to my list of problems isn't an option right now, so I take a deep breath and say as calmly as possible. "I'm going to pretend we never had this conversation. Now, I will say this only once. If you want Jasper to bail us out again, *you* ask him. I'm done with grovelling to my friend because you are bad at business. Now, wash your hands and call the boys. Dinner is ready."

Calmly, I lift the spoon and stir the dish in a weird catatonic state because it's as if something snapped inside me just then and set me free and I'm floating away from my problems. Enough is enough and I no longer want to try to patch something up that should have been laid to rest years ago. Daniel got us into this mess and as far as I'm concerned, it's up to him to get us out of it and even if we must sell our home, I'm never going to ask Amanda for anything again.

30
SAMANTHA

It's weird being home. I was only gone a few days and yet it's as if everything has changed. I reached an important decision in Dubai and the more I dwell on it, the more excited I am.

As I unpack, I wonder how I'll feel when I pack again, this time forever. If I am to be successful in this move, I must be both financially and mentally prepared.

Up until now, my life revolved around a man. When I fell in love with Ben, I was set for life. It wasn't easy being the wife of a soldier, but I threw myself into it with enthusiasm because I was in love. It took me a long time to fall out of love, but I believe I'm there now.

Now I love my job and myself and I have total control over that. I won't let myself down and if I work hard enough, I won't ever have to worry about money again.

As I make myself a mug of tea, I plan the next few days. Catch up with work and then start planning my brave new venture and as soon as I have the details, I'll send them to Ginny in the hope she comes with me. It won't be so bad if there are two of us and of all my friends, she is the only one I can see myself doing this with.

So, I am quite upbeat when I head to my desk and start work because right now, at this moment, I am in my happy place.

My mood evaporates quicker than an ice cube in a sauna when I see the email waiting for me halfway down the list. I almost don't want to open it, but curiosity wins. It's from Ben and I hate the flutter in my heart when I register his name, because why am I not over him yet?

Hey baby.
We need to talk. Can I swing by one evening?

What does he mean? We said everything in the days after he left. There can be no possible reason why we need to have a conversation, and yet I'm curious.

Sure. When were you thinking?

I'm a little surprised to receive his immediate response.

Are you free now?

My heart starts hammering because this is so sudden, and I'm not sure if I'm mentally prepared for a face-to-face meeting with him. It was one thing seeing him with his family in town, but having those astonishing blue eyes fixed on me will be a huge test of my emotions.

So, I type.

I'm a little busy today. What about next week?

I'm quite proud of myself because ordinarily I would be accommodating, and it's good to be assertive for once in my life.

Please Sammy, it's important.

Now my imagination is running riot, so I type back.

I can spare an hour this evening. Maybe meet at the Spotted Dog in town?

Thanks baby. I appreciate it. How about seven thirty?

Fine. See you then.

As the thread ends, my heart pounds and I'm ashamed of my reaction to him. It's been years since we last met and I can't think of any reason why he wants to meet up now. We didn't have the most amicable parting of the ways, and I was destroyed. It's taken me a long time to reach this point and the last thing I want is to be plummeted back into that dark place he left me in.

Benjamin Castle blew into my world like a cyclone and was every bit as devastating. He swept me off my feet and carried me along with him for the ride until the storm petered out. I was dropped from a great height and left bloodied, bruised, and broken on the ground and it's taken me a long time to build myself up again.

I like to believe I rebuilt myself stronger, but even the toughest structures are susceptible to damage and storms have a habit of returning and it's up to me to prepare my defences regarding this one.

I try to return to work, but I can't concentrate and hate the part of me that immediately wants to jump in the shower and make myself irresistible, just to show him what he's missing.

I use work to banish him from my mind and to a degree it works. As always, I'm busy solving other people's problems while I ignore my own.

Luckily, my mind is trained a lot better than my heart and takes over when I most need it and I spend the next few delicious hours wrapped up in my world of public relations where I plan my campaigns with a military precision.

I work for several clients who rely on me to spread the word about their products. Mainly virtual, which means I can take on clients anywhere in the world. I've always been good at social media, and I manage several profiles for businesses from Doggie clothing to fitness apps. I work for several authors mixed in with influencers who have grown such a large following they can no longer manage on their own. I charge a fixed fee and am even considering taking on an assistant so I can take on even more clients. My business is growing, and I love every minute of it, but even I know there is a ceiling to what I can offer.

Part of me hopes that Ginny would be up for learning my business because, like me, she is methodical and ruthless when setting goals. Her property management empire began at the local estate agents and moved online when the digital bubble exploded. Between us, we could help one another out and it's so important to me having her beside me when I move to a foreign country. It could be anywhere, but Dubai appeals because of the weather, the low crime rate, and the bonus that all my money would be tax free.

There is also an impressive ex-pat community and who knows, I may even find love again. Perhaps the romantic in me yearns for some excitement in my life, and what happened to Ginny in Dubai is the stuff of my fantasies.

Pushing all that away, I force myself to concentrate on business and try not to let the nerves affect me before my unexpected meeting tonight.

31
SAMANTHA

I'm not sure why I feel so nervous. It's as if I'm a kid meeting her crush for the very first time. Not my cheating ex-husband who really doesn't deserve *any* of my time, let alone causing me to agonise over what to wear to make myself look as amazing as possible.

I tell myself I'm doing it for myself. To raise my self-esteem and show him what he threw away for a shinier model.

However, I'm only kidding myself as my thoughts turn to his new girlfriend. Or is she his wife now? I never did find out, although it would be nice to know.

I lost touch with all our friends and his family when we

split up, and I was glad of it. I didn't want any reminders of Ben and his duplicity, and as much as I loved his parents, I couldn't bear to see their sympathetic looks while they stood firmly by his side.

My own family hate him with a passion and I'm almost positive they would be disappointed that I'm even here at all, but I'm curious. Who wouldn't be and so, with a deep breath, I head inside the Spotted Dog and prepare to meet the man I loved with all my heart for the first time in years.

As I enter the warm cosy atmosphere of the pub we used to come to a lot, it's as if the years melt away and I am right back where we started. The sage green walls and brown polished furniture are familiar, but the botanical prints and wooden floor are new. It appears to have had a makeover and is welcoming and warm, backed up by the roaring open fire that drives the chill away from the English winter.

"Sammy, over here."

I turn in the direction of the familiar voice and my heart lurches when I see Ben waving at me from a table by the window. It's almost as if the past few years melt away as I note his handsome, smiling face, those astonishing blue eyes sparkling across the room at me.

I fix a smile on my face, but inside I'm wrecked already. I thought I was stronger than this. Once again, I disappoint myself.

I head his way and fix a polite smile on my face, and he says warmly. "Thanks for coming. It's more than I deserve."

I merely nod and as I perch awkwardly on the edge of the chair, he pushes a large glass of white wine towards me and says softly, "I ordered your favourite. At least, it used to be."

For some reason, this small act of familiarity causes my eyes to fill with tears, which I blink angrily away and say with a sigh, "What's this about, Ben?"

He leans forward, causing me to shrink away, and he winces as he says apologetically, "I'm sorry, Sammy."

"You brought me here to apologise. What is it this time?" I snap back by way of a response.

The glass of wine remains untouched before me, and I notice his pint of lager is already half full, or is it half empty? The way my mind is working today, it prefers the latter.

"I've left Kate."

"Why does that concern me?" I shrug as if I'm completely unaffected, and he nods his agreement.

"It doesn't I suppose, but I've done a lot of thinking over the past few years and realise I treated you badly and I want to apologise for that."

"Then go ahead."

I fix him with a blank expression, and he nods in acceptance. "I deserve nothing from you, Sammy. The fact you turned up at all is more than I hoped for, but I want to apologise for cheating on you and then leaving you for somebody else."

"Is that it?" I'm being cold for a reason because inwardly my emotions are on fire, but he doesn't need to know that.

I have perfected the ice queen act since he left and from the look on his face, he is surprised by it.

"No."

"Go on." I leave the wine untouched and note he takes a huge swig of his own drink, telling me he's nervous, which surprises me. Ben was never the nervous type, and I wonder if there's something else.

"I'm due to return to active service."

"I never knew you left."

He nods. "A couple of years ago. Kate wanted me to spend more time with her and the kids and I took a desk job."

"Good for you." It hurts knowing he did something for her

that I begged him to do for me. Even now, it's painful that he put a virtual stranger's needs over mine.

"I was a fool, Sammy."

"For leaving active service?"

I gloss over the emotion that hangs between us because it's obvious he's trying to rewind the clock.

"No. For being blinded by lust and believing everything Kate told me."

I know I shouldn't be interested and should walk away now, but there's a part of me that's desperate to hear all the juicy details and relish in his misery. So, I say nothing and note his finger tapping nervously on his leg, something he always did when he was uncomfortable.

He says wearily, "I left you because Kate told me she was pregnant."

His words are like the sharpest knife carving open my heart because he knew I always wanted children and told me it wouldn't be fair to them. Their father could be killed any moment, and I would be left to raise them alone. Then the first woman who spread her legs trapped him in a far more devious way than I ever could and, if anything, I wish I had done the same. At least I would have had another human being to care for. Someone to love me unconditionally when nobody else did.

He interrupts my thoughts and says earnestly. "I wanted to do the right thing. When we discovered it was twins, I realised I had to walk away from our marriage and be responsible for once in my life. Those little girls needed a father and at first, I thought Kate was everything I ever wanted."

"At first?" I wait for the punchline, and he stares at me hard and whispers, "She wasn't. You see, one day when we were shopping at the mall, I caught a glimpse of you."

A shiver passes down my spine and my blood runs cold because I know exactly when that was.

"It hit me then."

"What did?"

"I was walking beside the wrong woman. My place was by your side and my life felt empty without you in it."

I grab the glass of wine and take a huge slug of alcohol to calm my raging heart, because I am really not strong enough to deal with this.

"I couldn't act on it, though. I had a new family, and I wasn't going to walk away from my responsibilities. Not a second time."

"But you did. You are." I say savagely and he winces as if I've stabbed him in the heart, not the other way around.

He shakes his head.

"It turns out they weren't my family after all."

I stare at him in shock and note the usually controlled man bend before my eyes as his eyes glitter with tears and he mumbles, "Kate told me she was pregnant before we met. Her ex was sent to prison, and she was scared and alone. I was the stupid fool waiting to be duped, and she told me it had been easy. Now her ex is back, and they want to be the family they really are, and she produced a DNA test backing up her story. All she wanted was a meal ticket, and she scored the jackpot with me."

I would say I'm sorry, but I'm not. The pain he put me through is hard to forgive and I suppose Karma had a hand in this and played a blinder.

He appears so broken and nothing like the man I married, and I suppose he has learned a valuable lesson from this.

Trying to be the bigger person, I say gently, "I'm sorry, Ben. Sorry that you were tricked and sorry that it didn't work out. Thanks for the apology, but forgiveness may take a little longer."

He nods. "I understand."

I make to stand, and he says quickly, "Please. Stay and have some supper with me. I leave tomorrow and, well, it's been a while."

I should leave while I'm still hanging onto my dignity, but there is something so familiar about being with Ben. A friendship that goes way back and a sense of belonging that I can't explain. So, I tell myself it's just one meal between two people, who, for a fleeting moment in time, shared their life before they both moved on to pastures new.

So, instead, I shrug out of my coat and paste a smile on my face and say softly, "Of course. It will be good to catch up."

32
GINNY

It's strange being home. I walked into a mountain of post which is unusual when it's only been a few days and a house that reminds me I forgot to leave the heating on. Cursing myself for attempting to combat the cost-of-living crisis, the first thing I do is race to my room to pull another jumper on.

I make myself a hot drink and sift through the post consisting mainly of flyers and useless advertising. I'm astonished that businesses still spend money on this when Sammy always said there were better forms of advertising.

However, there is one letter that looks official and with a sinking feeling, I open it with trembling fingers.

It's from my mortgage company telling me the interest rate is due to rise and as I note the figure, my heart drops and my head pounds. It's too much. Even though I was expecting it, I thought I would pay off the rest when the investment increased and then I could sell my shares in Daniel's development, pay off my mortgage, and put the rest into my pension.

Now I'm ruined and must face the possibility of selling my home and walking away with nothing to show for the past thirty years.

It's too much and only the phone ringing distracts me from a full-blown panic attack.

"Ginny, my love. Are you home yet?"

Omar.

For some reason, my eyes fill with tears at the sound of his reassuring voice.

"Yes." I steady my voice.

"I've just got home, and it's absolutely freezing here."

"Come and meet me."

"You're here?"

I'm amazed and he chuckles down the phone.

"My meeting in Saudi went well, and I brought forward my trip to London. I have a week before I must leave, and I want to spend it with you."

I feel like crying. This is just what I need and yet how can I switch off from the nightmare that is circling and threatening to pull me under?

He must sense my hesitation but says firmly, *"Take a cab to Riverside Gardens, Flat 306, in Chelsea. I'll pay the fare but make it here within the hour. I've missed you."*

"What now? I've just got in."

I attempt to laugh but it comes out as more of a sob and he says in a low voice, *"Don't make me come and get you."*

Then he cuts the call, leaving me conflicted.

On the one hand, I should be calling that cab immediately because I can't think of anything I want more right now and yet the grown-up part of my brain is telling me to take a moment and think through the position I'm in. I need to make a plan and I can't do that with my guilty pleasure between my legs and yet the wanton woman in me is winning this particular battle as I grab the phone and search for the nearest cab company.

Just one night.

That's all I'll take to place this nightmare on hold. After all, I can't achieve anything this evening anyway and I need the distraction the sexy Arab is promising me.

After just one hour, I am pressing the intercom of an apartment I never thought I'd be visiting.

It's a step up from the usual properties I manage and from a business point of view, I am salivating at the prestigious address and the possibility of one per cent commission on a sale that would run into millions.

On a personal level, I am eaten up with envy because who wouldn't want to live in a place like this? It's everything I ever wanted and as I wait for Omar to answer, I wonder about the man I have stumbled across in the most unexpected of ways.

The door opens and I head inside, clutching my coat around me defensively because I'm uncharacteristically nervous. In fact, it surprises me because I don't do nerves. I never have and yet, for some reason, this man brings them out in me.

Is it the unknown? The fact he's still a stranger and I'm walking into what could be a trap. It wouldn't be the first time I've done something foolish, but they are swept under the carpet and trodden down until they aren't even memories anymore. I celebrate my successes and banish my mistakes and I will never be any different. What remains to be seen is what category Omar falls into because I have never met a man like him.

I take the lift to the third floor and step out into a carpeted hallway and head in the direction of three hundred and six. My nerves are churning inside, wondering if it will be different here. Now I'm in my home country, all the reasons why I should walk away are screaming at me.

'He's a stranger. Run, don't walk. He could be a murderer, you stupid fool. He wants something from you that is probably illegal, and you could end up in prison.'

I battle through the red flags and reach his door and note it's open already.

I must have a long talk with my curiosity since it's heading up this mission and my common sense is nowhere to be found.

As I knock tentatively on the door, I hear the familiar voice of a stranger and I melt inside.

"Come in, Ginny."

I inch open the door, telling myself that if I don't like what I see I'll make a run for it, but I'm a fool because I definitely like what I see.

Omar is standing by the window, beside a table set for two, with London in the background as the most amazing vista. The table has been set with a white tablecloth on which the candles are flickering alongside a beautiful vase of red roses, creating a romantic atmosphere. Omar himself is mouth-watering and stares at me with a mixture of lust and friendliness. He is wearing black silk pants that hang low on his hips, his black t-shirt straining to contain the muscles of a man who visits the gym a lot. His dark glittering eyes stare across the room at me and in his hand is one of the red roses that he holds out to me in a sweet, romantic gesture.

"Welcome home, Ginny." He smiles, his perfect white teeth in direct contrast to his olive skin, and as I step inside, I drop my coat from my shoulders and smile provocatively.

"Welcome to London, Omar." I bat my lashes, feeling like a teenager again and as I take the rose with one hand, he grasps my other hand and pulls me flush against him. Then he kisses me slow, hard, and passionately and any doubts vanish in a haze of lustful intent.

If this is wrong, I'll deal with it in the morning because fantasies don't come true very often and I owe it to myself to indulge in this one for a little longer.

33
GINNY

As expected, our evening started in bed before we dragged ourselves out to enjoy the meal that Omar has provided. I say provided because it's obviously been prepared by a professional and was left in the oven until we had worked up a considerable appetite.

As we take our seats at the romantic table, he fills my glass with the most seductive red wine and raises a toast.

"To us."

"To us." I echo his words as I prepare to sample what smells divine while congratulating myself on my extremely good fortune.

"You say you're here for a week."

"I am." He nods as he pushes a forkful of food into his mouth and chews slowly, making my toes curl at the gleam in his eyes. I am fast realising that Omar was created from my lustful dreams because if I could have drawn a blueprint of my perfect man, it's him. I'm readying myself for the catch though and maintain an aloofness I need to hang onto.

"I would like us to spend it together."

He smiles and I nod happily. "I would love that, but I have to work, I'm afraid."

"What do you do?"

"Real estate. I run a company that sells to businesses mainly. I work out of the Richmond office, but it takes me all over London."

"You have a good career."

"It is, although..."

I'm unsure whether to tell him of my plans and my voice trails off, causing him to raise his eyes. "Although what?"

"I've had an offer I'm thinking of accepting."

"Which is?"

"To move to Dubai, actually," He raises his eyes and I grin.

"One of the friends I went with is moving her business there and said I should do the same. Search for a job selling property over there or set up on my own."

"That sounds interesting."

He sips his wine, looking thoughtful and I nod with a little more enthusiasm. "The trouble is, it's come at a tricky time."

"Why?"

I'm in two minds whether to say anything or not because Omar is still a stranger and doesn't know my situation, so I decide to share the burden a little and say sadly, "I made a bad investment and now my home is at risk. My friend said I should rent it out and go to Dubai to help pay off the mortgage and when I come back to England, I will still have an asset."

"She's a wise friend."

Omar runs his finger around the rim of his glass thoughtfully and then says in his deep, sexy voice.

"What was the investment?"

"One of the friends I was with is married to a financial guy. Stocks and shares, you know the type."

He raises his eyes, which causes me to giggle because he doesn't just know the type, he *is* the type.

It encourages me to offload my problem onto him because he may be able to help, and I say with a sigh. "He told me it was a sure-fire investment. Buy when they are low and sell when they are high. He assured me we were in at the beginning and when we sold, we could triple our investment."

"And you believed him." Omar shakes his head, which doesn't make me feel any better, and I nod. "We grew up together. He's married to one of my closest friends. Why wouldn't I believe him?"

I'm a little defensive, probably because I was so foolish, and Omar nods as if he understands.

"So, tell me what happened?"

"It was a property investment in a plot overseas. Italy actually. It was planned to be a development with two hotels and apartments, shops, and bars. It was huge, and the land was cheap."

I take a swig of my wine and say sadly, "Then the diggers unearthed something of historical significance and the site was shut down – permanently. The development crashed, and any money invested is being used to pay off any debts owed."

"What is the name of this development?"

Omar's eyes have narrowed to dangerous slits, and a shiver runs down my spine.

"Hades."

He raises his eyes. "More like hell."

I nod miserably. "I've lost everything, and I feel like such a failure."

To my surprise, he reaches across the table and entwines his fingers with mine.

"Look at me, Ginny."

I raise my eyes to his and witness the flashing anger of a man who surprises me more every time I see him, and he growls, "I will deal with this for you."

"How?" I'm astonished and he says with determination.

"It's what I do. What I'm good at and many of my contacts can find the information we need."

"We?"

My heart leaps at his choice of words and he smiles.

"We, Ginny. We are together for as long as you say we are."

"I don't understand."

It's all happening so quickly, and Omar raises my hand to his lips and kisses it gallantly before saying huskily, "Nobody likes to be alone, my angel. We may find ourselves in that position, but it's wrong. I have never married, choosing to marry my career, I suppose. I've dated many women who don't understand my needs."

Now I'm afraid and say with a catch to my voice. "Needs?"

"Freedom."

He stares into my eyes and says firmly, "I work. It's the most important thing in my life and my private life comes second. I don't want a family and never have. Over the years, the women I met have told me they are fine with that, but after a while, they grow unhappy when they want more than what I am willing to give. We are not young anymore. We are past the age of having a family and now I have made millions I want to share them with someone. But not my freedom."

"What are you saying?" I am genuinely confused, and he rubs his thumb on the back of my hand and stares deep into my eyes.

"I want someone to be there when I am available and, in return, I will be loyal. I never cheat and I expect the same from my partner. We don't live together, and we don't have friends. There will be no attending family gatherings and when we are together, there will be no distractions."

"That sounds…cold."

I'm shocked to say that out loud because surely that sounds like my ideal relationship, and he shrugs. "That is why I am alone and searching for a similar free spirit. Someone who shares their life with me when I'm in town, whenever that will be. Occasionally, we will travel together on holidays, business trips and extended breaks. Then we return to our own lives until we meet again with no recriminations and demands on our time. I will treat you like a queen when I am around, and you will want for nothing. To prove that I will help you with your problem. Email the details and I will look into it and if there is another way, I will find it for you."

"You would do that?"

I'm astonished and he nods. "I *can* do that. It's what I do and if there is any way out of this for you, it will be my greatest pleasure in finding it."

My eyes fill with surprising tears because nobody ever helps me. I've always dealt with everything on my own and I'm not used to this.

Then there's his proposition. It shocked me and I'm not sure what I think about it, really. If anything, it sounds so cold, yet is it any different to how I've operated all these years? Dating apps and one-night stands are a little demeaning for a woman plunging headfirst into the menopause.

Could Omar be the answer to my prayers, or a welcome distraction to finding my real happily ever after?

I'm not sure what I think and as if he senses my hesitation, he smiles and then winks, which scatters my resistance like oil on water. "I see you need further persuasion, my darling."

I swear every part of me melts when he looks at me like that and I say breathlessly, "I'm open to persuasion."

He stands and, keeping my hand in his, leads me back to carry on where we left off earlier.

34
SONIA

One week later, and I am running out of excuses for Samantha. She messages most days, telling me politely that the money still hasn't come through. Every time I assure her it's been sent, and she should wait for it to register in her bank.

I never sent the money.

I don't have any and I feel like the worst friend in the world.

Come to think of it, I haven't been the best of friends to any of them. When I look back on our relationship over the years, I'm ashamed of my behaviour.

I've had a long time to think these past few days due to

the fact I can't go out because I have no money to spend. I don't want to talk to anyone because what would I say? If anything, I'm ashamed of myself because of what I've become.

I stare out of my patio doors onto the garden and note the first sign of spring pushing up through the damp, sodden earth, promising new beginnings and fresh starts.

If only my life was so easy. Even now I will do anything to hold on to the dream. To be one of the mums that the others wish they were. To enjoy a life many envies and be the person others look up to.

There is no point towering above everyone on a pedestal because it's a lonely place. The trouble is, I can't bear the humiliation of dropping down to join them. To be the recipient of the pitying gazes that used to glance up at me with admiration. I can't be that person and I won't be. Daniel's right. I need to step up and save this family once again!

My hand physically shakes when I reach for my phone and the bottle of gin I hid in my wardrobe is calling to me right now. The fact I haven't touched a drop of alcohol for two days is starting to affect me and the demon drink is a very real ghost right now as it haunts my every waking hour.

The trouble is, when Daniel so kindly highlighted my guilty pleasure, it shocked me a little. Referring to it as a drink problem at all made me stop and think and come to the damning conclusion he's right.

In fact, I've probably known for quite some time and I'm ashamed of myself. I made a vow that night to step up and be bigger than that. To deal with my problems in a grown-up way and face them head on. I've tried so hard to keep busy under the pressure, but at times like this I need to get courage from somewhere.

I stare at the phone and hesitate above Amanda's name. I

can't believe it's come to this. Afraid to call my best friend because of what I have done. What I've always done. I've treated her so badly I can't even live with myself and no wonder she snapped.

The fact this has gone on for close to thirty years now makes any excuses null and void. I've used her in a way I'm not proud of and I'm just shocked she put up with it for so long.

The first time I borrowed money from her, I couldn't believe it was so easy. She just smiled and asked how much and transferred the money while I waited. That first payment was one thousand pounds, and I assured her I would pay it back with interest. I meant it back then, and it never occurred to me I would never pay it back.

However, she waved it away and called it a gift and I accepted it gratefully.

I should have stopped then. Paid her back and never asked again, but it became addictive.

She would offer to pay when we went out, and I thanked her. She shook her head when I offered my share, and I told myself she owed me. To settle my conscience, I told myself that if it wasn't for me, she wouldn't be in that position which is right. Then again, why should she pay me for something that happened by chance, anyway?

Then we had kids and Daniel started buckling under the pressure. He couldn't cope, and the handouts became a lifeline. Just ten thousand to pay the mortgage arrears. Twenty thousand to pay the boy's school fees. When I think of the money, I demanded, I want to cower under my bed.

We should have paid it back instead of spending any money Daniel earned on bonuses. Trips abroad, brand new cars and a hot tub. All the time Amanda would smile and appear happy for me, but I've noticed over the years that smile has faded and been replaced by a thin line of disapproval.

A few years ago, she broached the subject and asked if I was going to pay her back. I made her feel terrible for asking. I turned it around on her and ignored her for days. I never called and arranged trips out with my school friends, hoping she would find herself on the edge of the group.

When she called, she never mentioned it again, and we carried on as normal. She paid my share for everything, and it became our arrangement.

Now I must ask her again and once again, our future depends on it and despite my brave words to Daniel when I returned home, I always knew I would be back here doing the same thing to save our family. So, with a deep breath, I make the call.

She answers almost immediately,

"Sonia."

I note the guarded tone to her voice, and I say cheerfully, "What's up? We haven't spoken since Dubai. Do you fancy a coffee?"

This has always been my tried and tested solution to every problem by ignoring it and carrying on as before. Most of the time it works because I am the only friend Amanda has and she knows it.

"Sure. Do you want to come here?"

"Great. I'll be there within the hour."

I cut the call because I'm liable to burst out crying. I can't believe I'm doing this and yet even though I know it is wrong, I'm going, anyway.

I paint a brave smile on my face and ignore the sound of the gin bottle calling me and head out to my car, hoping there's enough petrol in the tank for the trip.

Sonia and Jasper live down a private track, and I've always envied their immense property that sits surrounded by landscaped gardens and an orchard where fruit trees are in abundance. There's a triple garage with brand new top of the range cars that they trade in every three years for the newest model. Their house has a guest cottage in the grounds that Jasper's father lives in and he helps maintain the property in return for his keep.

They built an Olympic sized swimming pool and two hot tubs. A pool house with a bar and a snooker table inside. We have enjoyed many parties at Amanda's and Jasper's and every time I wished it was my life.

Inside is no different. Huge rooms that are tastefully decorated and equipped with every luxury on the market. They built a home cinema in the basement and a huge gym in the attic. Amanda and Jasper enjoy separate dressing rooms and their kitchen is the biggest I have ever seen. Somehow, everything ties together to create a happy family home and I've always told myself that the money she gives me is a drop in their ocean. They won't miss it; it won't affect their lives in any way and it's what friends do after all. They help one another.

That is why I said I would come here, because this makes everything I ask acceptable. To me, anyway.

So, as I park my own leased car, I prepare my mind to save my family at the expense of my friendship.

35
SONIA

I follow Amanda into her huge kitchen and note the frostiness in the atmosphere. I noticed it as soon as she opened the door, and my heart is beating so fast as I follow her inside and hope she thaws out a little.

"How have you been?" She enquires as she lifts the kettle and fills it from the tap, and I smile as if I haven't got a care in the world.

"Good thanks. Dubai was amazing, wasn't it?"

"Yes." She switches on the kettle and lifts some shortbread from a glass jar in her pantry cupboard and places them on a plate that she slides across the marble counter towards me.

"Have you heard from the others?" I'm curious because aside from Samantha, I've haven't, and she shakes her head. "No, but that's not unusual."

It reminds me how I arrange everything, which almost makes me believe I earn her money, and I say with a sigh. "Daniel's so worried about the investment. We both are."

"I'm sure you are." She heaps coffee into two mugs, and I say quickly, "I mean, I'm sure it's just a blip, really. Actually, Daniel wants to bend Jasper's ear about it. Do you think he'll be up for that?"

"I can ask." She pours the coffee into the mugs and the aroma hits my senses, reminding me of many similar chats over the years.

"Why don't we meet up one evening? You could come to dinner." I say hopefully and she nods. "I'll ask Jasper. Evenings are difficult because he works so late."

"Of course." I shift in my seat, noting her cool manner when she is normally so warm and welcoming.

I try to make polite conversation and say, "How are the kids?"

"Fine, thank you. Freddie is busy captaining the school football team and Saskia is studying for her GCSEs. India is heading to Paris on work experience at a couture house the school has set up."

"Wow, what an opportunity." I'm impressed and once again it reminds me how different life is when you have money. Their kids went to the most expensive schools and received a far superior education to mine, despite the fact they also attended private schools. Even then there are tiers and as hard as I tried, we never quite reached the top one.

"Did you send Samantha her money?" Amanda surprises me by saying and I shift in my seat.

"It's a little tricky."

"What is?"

Now I have my opening and I say sadly, "Daniel is struggling, and our credit has been put on hold. I don't have the resources to send it to her, but he assures me it's a temporary thing and as soon as he untangles the consortium mess, things will be rosy again."

"I see." She smiles. "That's good. At least he has a plan."

"He does." I reply brightly, waiting for her to offer to pay Samantha for me.

"So, how are the boys? Did they miss you?"

"Of course not." I roll my eyes, causing her to grin, and I could almost believe we are friends again.

As Amanda pushes the coffee towards me, she says apologetically. "I'm sorry, Sonia, I have a lunch appointment with Bethany at the country club. I must leave in twenty minutes. I hope you understand."

"Bethany?" This is the first time I've heard her name and Amanda nods. "Yes, we attend Pilates together on Tuesdays. She's so much fun. You would like her."

"I'm sure." I sip my coffee, noting a sudden change in the atmosphere. It's almost as if the tide is turning and Amanda is the popular one, not me.

She glances at her watch and says with an apologetic smile. "I don't have long, but it was good to catch up. Let me know when you want to meet up for that meal. I'll bring a bottle."

I'm hoping she'll bring a lot more than that, but I realise when I'm beaten and so I smile and stand, my unfinished coffee pushed to one side.

"Of course. Well, enjoy you lunch with Bethany."

"We always do."

She walks beside me to the door, and there's a sense of

unease brewing. I've been replaced already, and I don't like how that makes me feel.

———

On the way home, I think long and hard about my friendship with Amanda and I don't like my part in it. She has always been the best friend I ever had and has always been there for me. From growing up to meeting and marrying our partners. We had our children at the same time and enjoyed bringing them up together.

Through all those years I took but never gave back. I realise that now and I don't mean financially. I only saw her when it suited me, despite the times she asked to meet up when she was at a loose end. I never listened to her problems, preferring to bend her ear on mine and it's only now I'm faced with losing her that I appreciate everything I had.

———

Tonight will be special for a variety of reasons.

My visit to Amanda's home was three days ago, and we've arranged for them to dine with us this evening. I've tried so hard to make it special with extremely limited resources and created a warm and cosy atmosphere and banished the boys to their friends. There is a lot riding on tonight and it's important to build a few bridges and move mountains because our future as friends depends on it.

———

Amanda and Jasper pull up on the driveway at seven thirty and I open the door with Daniel by my side and welcome them as if there is nothing unusual about this evening at all.

Amanda is wearing a black trouser suit, her Gucci bag draped around her shoulder and her jewellery sparkling in the glare of the porch lighting.

Jasper is casual in jeans and a checked shirt. A blue blazer offering the only nod to formality, and he is holding a bottle of champagne and flowers that obviously didn't come from the local petrol station.

"Guys, it's so good to see you." I fawn over them with a flakiness that makes me wince inside.

A lot is riding on tonight and it's important not to mess this up and as the men walk into the living room, I pull Amanda along with me to the kitchen.

"Thanks, Amanda. I don't deserve a friend like you." I gush as I open the bottle of champagne they brought with them.

"What's brought this on?" She enquires, appearing confused, and I sigh.

"I realise Daniel can be a little well, eager, and this is probably the last thing Jasper wants to be doing in his spare time."

"It's fine." Amanda shrugs and says with a smile. "In three months, he will have a lot more of it."

"What do you mean?" I'm stunned and she grins.

"He's taking early retirement. He's giving up work to devote his time to us instead."

I stare at her in amazement, and she chuckles softly. "I had the same expression when he told me. The day we returned from Dubai as it happens. I'm so happy though, and we can finally do all the things we talked about."

The radiance in her expression tells me she's serious and I

experience the usual pang of envy when I witness my friend's good fortune. While we are fighting to save our livelihood, they are preparing to enjoy theirs and it doesn't make me feel any better about our situation.

Pushing my jealously aside, I plaster a smile on my face. "I'm happy for you. It's been a long time coming."

"It has."

She sips her champagne and says with a smile. "Who knew it would all work out so well in the end?"

36
AMANDA

The expression on Sonia's face is priceless. She is trying so hard to disguise her jealously while appearing the supportive friend. However, thirty years have counted for something, and I can read every thought in her head right now and it's not happiness. Jealousy, bitterness, and disappointment. I'm guessing they are what she's experiencing now and I'm enjoying every second of this because, despite everything we've been through, I deserve this, and I won't let her tell me otherwise.

Dinner turns out to be an awkward dance of dodging the real issue we're here, and it's as if a wall has been built between us. I wish things had been different. Money has got in the way of what should have been a good friendship, and I'm not sure when it all started to go wrong. It crept up on me so gradually I got used to it before I noticed it was a problem at all and as I watch the anxious looks Sonia and Daniel share when they think we're not looking, I almost change my plan. Almost.

The trouble with Sonia is she's always been the friend who stabs me and then pretends she's bleeding. Her feelings have always taken precedence over mine, and I wonder why I ever thought that was acceptable.

The conversation changes from polite chit chat to more serious matters after the main course and as Sonia heads to the kitchen to bring in the dessert, Daniel says casually, "I could use your help with the Hades consortium. It's a mess."

Jasper nods, appearing thoughtful, and my heart jumps as a surge of affection for my husband hits me. Even now he is interested, keen to help, despite knowing that he's being used again.

Sonia heads back into the room holding a glass bowl filled with trifle as Jasper says, "Amanda told me what happened, and I had a look into the company."

I swear you could hear a pin drop as Sonia sets the bowl on the table and sits down silently, regarding Jasper as if he's about to reveal the ten commandments. For some reason a wave of immense pity hits me for my friend and placing myself in her designer shoes, I realise it can't have been easy all these years. The constant worry about whether Daniel will mess up again, not only at work but also in their relationship. As I steal a glance at the man himself, I discover a resentful hatred for a man who only ever considered his own wishes, despite his wife fighting so hard to keep their marriage alive.

"Hades was set up by a company who invested in similar developments worldwide." Jasper says conversationally.

"They secured the investment but on further investigation discovered there were concerns about the historical value of the land, so they decided to pull out and placed their shares on the market, trying to recover some of their losses and move onto the next project."

I watch Daniel keenly and he nods as if he already knows this, and Jasper leans forward and says with some excitement. "It appears those shares were bought up quite quickly because the news wasn't common knowledge. For a while everything went ahead and then another investor entered the game and bought up most of the shares."

Daniel nods. "Yes, and pulled out, causing the share price to fall and then the news of the historical nature of the site rendered the rest worthless."

Jasper nods. "That's true, but on further investigation, it appears the history was disclosed months before the crash. Any capable manager would have discovered this and moved accordingly. It's almost as if they were manipulating the markets for their own gain."

I stare at Daniel, who appears to be a little redder than before and Sonia appears confused but says nothing, just waiting for the punchline that tells her everything will be ok in the end.

Jasper says with a huge sigh. "I also heard the entire project is being investigated by the professional standards committee, which is a problem for everyone involved."

Daniel interrupts quickly. "It's normal practice."

He smiles reassuringly at his wife, but she appears worried, and she has good cause to be.

Jasper leans forward and says casually, "It doesn't help your investors, but I know of something that might."

This time Daniel leans forward and all I can hear is his heavy breathing as he says quickly, "I'm listening."

Jasper nods. "There's a company that isn't trading particularly well at the moment and has a low share value. By chance, when I was reading the small print of a trade magazine, a small article caught my eye. The owner has been diagnosed with terminal cancer and doesn't have long. The article was about a pioneering drug they were trialling, and he was interviewed in relation to that. I recognised the name and did some digging and discovered he has no sons or daughters to carry on the family business. Without him, the company will fail unless he finds a buyer."

I swear every person in the room is hanging on his every word, me included as I sense everything changing and Jasper says with a smile, "I had a word with one of my colleagues who works in that field, and he's interested."

"So, the share price could double when he buys the company. Is that what you're saying?"

Daniel's eyes light up with greed, and Jasper nods. "Yes. Buy now and sell when the announcement is made. The company concerned is a major player and would do well out of the investment. Everyone is happy."

Daniel nods, his eyes swivelling to Sonia's, who is a walking advertisement for relief right now.

"The trouble is, you need money to invest."

Jasper shakes his head as if it's case closed.

Daniel says quickly, "We can get the money."

He peers at Sonia and completely disregards the startled shock on her face as he says with excitement.

"We have this house."

"No, Daniel." She says emphatically, and he whispers from the corner of his mouth. "You heard Jasper, it's a certainty. We would be fools not to invest."

He says quickly, "What do you suggest?"

Jasper says carefully, "I'm suggesting nothing. I'll tell you the details and the decision will be yours if decide to invest or not. I must warn you though, there is always risk involved and I'm only telling you what I know."

"Are you investing?"

Sonia interrupts and Jasper nods. "I would be a fool not to. I have moved several of my clients' portfolios around to accommodate this investment and in a private capacity I am also in."

Sonia nods and says with determination, "Then we're in."

As she dips the serving spoon in the trifle, my heart beats so fast I wonder if they can hear it. Now the trap has been set. I'm surprised to find I'm disgusted with myself. I know it's for the very best reason there is, but it doesn't make me feel any better. They say revenge is sweet. I disagree. It's a bitter pill to swallow and I don't really like myself right now.

We make our excuses soon after dessert and as we head home, I say with confusion. "I still don't understand how this will get everyone their money back?"

Our plan was to pay everyone back what they had lost through Daniel, ourselves included, and Jasper says grimly, "Daniel won't be able to re-mortgage the house."

"Why not?"

I'm surprised because he seemed pretty sure about that.

"He already did."

"And Sonia doesn't know."

I'm shocked and Jasper nods. "Daniel re-mortgaged his house to invest in Hades. He set up a fake company and used Ginny's and Connor's money as an investment in that."

"I still don't understand."

Jasper says angrily, "When I did my research, I discovered a company called Summerhouse holdings. The director is listed as Sonia Sullivan and shareholders are Connor Bailey and Ginny Edwards. The value of the company was one million pounds that was lost when the Hades consortium folded."

"Do you think Sonia knows?" I'm horrified and Jasper says grimly, "I doubt it. The company was formed just before it crashed and was probably done online by Daniel. He would have got Sonia to sign the paperwork and probably told her it was something else entirely, or more likely forged her signature. He would have access to her personal documents, and if I know Daniel, he kept it to himself."

"Wow. So, what does that mean?"

Jasper chuckles softly. "It means that Summerhouse holdings may well get their money back."

I slump back in my seat and shake my head in confusion.

"This is why I ferry kids to clubs. It's way over my head."

He reaches across and grasps my knee and whispers, "Trust me, darling. I have it all under control and nobody will ever discover what we've done."

As we head home, I hope that's true because I'm not currently feeling very good about myself. For all her faults, Sonia has been a friend to me over the years and I don't want to see her lose everything, even though it was never hers to lose in the first place. Daniel has made so many bad decisions over the years it affected us all and it had to stop somewhere. If we can pull this off and leave everyone happy, it will be a bloody miracle.

37
CATHERINE

I am so nervous. I can't believe I'm doing this at all, especially not the day after I called time on my marriage.

When things ended with Connor, I was exhilarated, which was an emotion I wasn't expecting at all. Sadness perhaps, grief, worry and despair, but never exhilaration.

I expect it's the shock. Tomorrow may be different, but for now I'm excited. Connor and I talked well into the night. I listened to his reasoning but couldn't accept it. It struck me that we existed more as acquaintances than lovers. We certainly weren't friends and the way he has treated me for several years now can't be forgotten in a hurry.

We slept in separate rooms, and he was out before I woke. A practical note on the kitchen counter telling me he was heading to Manchester on business and would be away for three days and that maybe I should use the time to calm down and think about what is best for Sally and our family.

If anything, it made me even more determined to end this marriage because, even faced with his own guilt he is trying to make me feel bad. For what? Over twenty years of dedication, loyalty, and love. Trying to make something work that was obvious a few years on from our marriage that it wasn't working.

So, I have three days to change my life. It makes me giggle when I picture it as a film title. But this is no fabricated story for entertainment. This is *my* life and for once I am going to do something I would be scared of before. I'm going to tuck my wedding ring into my jewellery box and head out on a blind date. Just because I can.

———

Parmigiana is an Italian restaurant about a thirty-minute drive away and for the entire ride over, I've had second thoughts. The nerves have almost turned my car around several times and my heart has danced a guilty tango all the way here.

The fact I'm smartly dressed and styled my hair is unusual. I almost forgot I had a dress because leggings and sweatshirts have been my best friends for more years than I care to remember. I'm not ready to show the world the many curves I'm hiding, but when I tried on a dress I bought with next day delivery, I had to fight back my tears when I saw myself as the woman I had drifted away from years ago.

The clothes act like a shield because I feel amazing. I have really tried, and I hope it was worth it.

I edge inside the restaurant and note the dark, intimate atmosphere and swallow hard when the waitress peers up and smiles.

"May I help you?"

"I, um..." The words stick in my throat because what am I doing here and yet before I can turn and run, a low voice by my ear says, "Cathy, I'm sorry I'm late."

I turn to stare at my side swipe and immediately recognise the rather rugged features of Jack Bennett, minus his Labrador. I instantly relax at the warmth from the twinkle in his eye and his slightly crooked smile of apology as he leans in and whispers, "I don't know about you, but I'm uncharacteristically nervous."

I nod and say with a shy smile, "Me too."

He drops me a wink and turning to the waitress, says pleasantly, "Jack Bennett. We have a reservation for seven thirty."

She consults her list and then nods, grabbing two menus from the desk.

"Of course, follow me." She says brightly and Jack hangs back as I follow her through what I am sure are the curious stares of our fellow diners. They must realise I'm a married woman secretly seeing someone I met on the internet. It's probably written all over my face and I should be told to leave at once. The fact the restaurant is in a place I have never been before is reassuring, but what if someone recognises me?

My heart is thumping as she shows us to a table set in the corner and I'm glad to sink down in my chair with my back to the restaurant. At least I can hide now. Hopefully until everyone else has left because what am I thinking?

Jack takes his seat opposite and smiles as the waitress hands us both a menu and says she'll be back to take our drinks order.

Jack says in a low voice, "This is pretty scary, don't you think?"

"I do." I offer him a nervous smile and he says politely. "I'm Jack and you are Cathy, and we are doing nothing wrong. At least I hope we're not." He regards me with a quizzical grin, and I say in a rush. "No, we're not, but I must tell you one thing before we continue."

Now he looks worried, and I say in a whisper, "I am married but, well, recently separated."

"Recently?" He says with a raised brow and I say apologetically. "Yesterday."

The shock on his face causes me to say quickly, "Please don't think badly of me. It took a short trip away with my friends to realise my marriage ended years ago. The fact I was dreading going home told me that and, well, if I'm honest, the relationship ended some time ago, but neither of us would admit it."

He smiles, but I can tell he's shaken, and I say quickly, "I'll understand if you want me to leave. I just wanted to tell you because, well, you are the first man I've met since my husband over twenty-five years ago. The fact I downloaded the app was a big step that I needed to take to pull me out of my comfort zone."

Jack shakes his head and says slowly, "My wife died three years ago. Just before she died, I discovered she was having an affair with my best friend. I lost them both within two days of finding out and it's taught me one thing."

I don't know what to say. I'm so shocked and he says sadly, "That shit happens, and you need to push it aside and not dwell on it. Life's too short and you don't have time to waste on things that no longer work."

"I'm so sorry." I genuinely am because Jack appears a decent guy and he shrugs. "It had been going on for ten years. I felt like a fool. The entire time my life was a lie and I never even got to hear the full story. She told me on her death bed and then asked for my forgiveness."

"Oh my God! What did you say?" I am so sorry for the man sitting before me and he shrugs. "I had no choice. Of course, I told her I forgave her, she was dying and was obviously setting things right, in her conscience, anyway."

"Did you though?"

I'm intrigued, and he shakes his head.

"No. I was angry. Hurt. Broken. I was in pain from losing my wife, who I still had feelings for despite being angry with her, and I had to accept her death at the same time. Play the grieving husband in front of our family and friends all the time knowing our marriage was built on a lie."

"It must have been incredibly painful."

He nods. "It happened three years ago, and it's taken me every single one to reach this point."

"And the first person you meet lands a truth bomb on you that must have you questioning that decision."

I am mortified and then startled when he leans forward and says in a low whisper, "It makes me like you even more."

"Why?"

I'm shocked and he smiles sadly. "I appreciate your honesty. It's something I value, especially after the lies my wife told. If anything, I admire you. It can't have been easy to admit that, and if you want to talk about it, I'm a good listener."

Just like that any doubts evaporate and as the waitress

returns and asks for our drink order, we fall into an easy friendship as we order like any other couple, any concerns firmly drowned in shock and a desire to test the water a little and see where this date takes us.

38

CATHERINE

Jack Bennett is exactly what I needed. I can't remember spending such a pleasant evening in years. It was as if I was meeting an old friend and he has an easy conversation that keeps us talking until the restaurant closes.

As he walks me to my car, I'm nervous because I'm not sure what happens next. However, he merely steps forward and kisses me lightly on both cheeks before saying softly, "I had a great evening, Cathy. We should do it again soon."

His eyes twinkle in the lamplight and I'm experiencing a sense of loss already that the evening is over and we must go our separate ways and I say with a smile, "I'd love that. I had a good time."

"Me too."

He nods. "Text me when things settle down at home. I'll understand if you don't. No hard feelings."

"Why wouldn't I?" I say carefully and he shrugs. "Your situation is fresh. Still raw and when your husband comes home, you may have second thoughts. I just want to say that if you decide to call it a day on your marriage, there is a friend waiting who would love to see you again."

"Thank you."

I don't know what else to say and he says brightly, "Have a safe journey home."

I nod and as I step into my car, he turns and walks away, and I stare after him hoping this isn't the last I'll see of Jack Bennett. There is something between us that demands another chance and perhaps it's because it's new and forbidden, or perhaps it's because sometimes in life you get somewhere early before you should and that's exactly how I feel about him. It's too early to meet someone else. I understand that, but fate has delivered an opportunity I am keen to explore.

As I start the engine and the radio kicks in, my heart skips a beat when I hear, 'You belong with me', by Taylor Swift. Is it a sign, an omen perhaps? I shouldn't be smiling now. I should be wracked with guilt and scurrying home to beg for my husband's forgiveness. What would he say if he knew where I was now and what about Sally? She doesn't deserve this. I'm a mother with responsibilities, not a carefree teenager with no problems and all the time in the world.

Then again, perhaps that's why I'm doing this. I *don't* have all the time in the world anymore. My best days are behind me, and I devoted them to a man I've known for many years didn't deserve them. What about me and what I want?

Do I still matter, or should my own desires and needs be pushed aside to make way for my family's?

I am so conflicted and yet note a strange lightness to my spirit that wasn't there before meeting Jack.

We've both been disappointed by our partners, but nothing can be worse than watching a loved one die, whatever they've done. He must have been so angry and yet still took three years to grieve for his past relationship. He took his time, something I'm conscious of. I should let this be the last time we meet and devote the rest of my life to making my marriage work. I should do the right thing, but what if the right thing on this occasion goes by the name of Jack Bennett?

―――

When Connor returns after a few days in Manchester, he walks into the house as if nothing happened at all. He slings down his briefcase and says with an irritated sigh, "The traffic was murder. I could use a gin and tonic."

He doesn't even grace me with a smile and just stomps off to the shower as he usually does, expecting the drink he ordered to be waiting for him. It's not.

When he returns, I'm preparing dinner as I've done for the past twenty-five years, and his irritated expression makes me smile as he registers he must fix his own drink if he wants it.

"I see you're still mad." He grumbles, causing me to stare at him in amazement.

"This isn't just an argument, Connor. This is the end of our marriage. Or had you forgotten that?"

He shrugs. "It doesn't have to be."

"What do you mean? Of course, it has to be. You slept

with another woman in our bed, not to mention the fact you gambled away our life savings and we are facing destitution."

"You're so melodramatic; you always have been."

He says with a heavy sigh. "Look, I realise I messed up, and I'm not proud of sleeping with Callie."

"Is that her name? I'm surprised you even asked." I retort with bitterness, and he shakes his head as if I'm the one who disappointed him.

"I understand you're angry and I suppose you have every right."

"You suppose!"

I can't believe this conversation, and he nods. "You must accept some of the blame for this."

"What have I done?" I yell, the frustration bubbling up to the surface as I face him with my eyes blazing.

"I've done nothing but put up with your moods for more years than I can remember. I've tip-toed around inside our marriage, telling myself this is how it's supposed to be. You have always called the shots and expected me to fall into line and the moment my back is turned, you screw someone else behind it. Was that the first time or have you been doing it for years? It would certainly explain why we don't anymore."

He looks so shocked it almost makes me giggle, and then a huge wave of sadness hits me as I listen to myself.

So, I set the knife down and wiping my hands on the tea towel, I step away from the counter. Then, moving across the room, I reach for the bottle of wine and pour myself a huge glass, before saying casually, "I'm done with fighting. Whatever your reasons were, I really don't care anymore."

"You don't." He appears a little stunned at that and I nod, weariness etching my words as the tears sparkle behind my eyes.

"Whatever happened brought us to this point, and it was inevitable."

I sit at the table and am surprised when he joins me and for a moment we just sit in silence as our marriage crashes and burns around us. Two people who met, fell in love, and married. Had a child and then grew apart. Both struggling to do the right thing rather than admit failure and move on, making one another miserable in the process.

"Tell me about the investment." I change the subject and Connor says with a heavy sigh. "Daniel came to me and told me it was too good to miss. We could triple our money in as many months, and that was one hell of a carrot to dangle in front of my face."

"And now?"

I sip my wine and he groans. "He called me yesterday and said the game was up and there was no hope of getting our money back."

"Do you believe him?"

"I must. I did my own research, and the land is all over the local news over there. It's legit and our money is being used to pay for the creditors who had already started on the work."

"There must be some left?"

"It was all tied up in shares, which devalued and are now worth nothing. We've lost it all."

He appears so dejected and nothing like his normal self, and in this moment, I experience a pang of sympathy for him. I suppose he did nothing wrong. If anything, he trusted a friend and wanted to make more money than we have enjoyed until this point.

I say in a gentler voice, "So, where do we go from here?"

"That's up to you."

"Me?"

"Yes." He appears a little lost, which throws me for some reason and then he sighs heavily. "I wasn't honest with you, Cathy."

Dread curls its icy fingers around my heart and I whisper, "I don't understand."

My voice shakes a little because how much more can a woman take?

"Callie."

"What about her?"

"I didn't just pick her up that night."

I stare at him in a frozen state of shock as he says casually. "We've been having an affair for three years. We met at the golf club. I lied when I said she was a prostitute. I don't know why I said that. I suppose I thought it sounded better somehow. Emotionless even and not as much of a betrayal."

I'm speechless because for a second there I felt sorry for him.

He takes my silence as a good sign and says almost conversationally.

"We didn't mean for it to happen. I suppose one taste was all it took to fuel the craving. Anyway, we normally meet at her house. She's got her own company and is quite wealthy in her own right. It was exciting, forbidden even, and our marriage had stalled, and I was vulnerable."

I want to punch him so badly and I'm not sure if he realises how 'vulnerable' he is to that right now, and I stare at him with pure hatred boiling inside.

"Anyway, when you went on your trip, she was curious about our home, so I brought her here. I never meant for us to end up in our bed, but we had too much to drink, and things escalated."

I'm numb with horror because this is far worse than I first

thought and he says with a slight shake of the head, "So, now you know. It's a good thing it's come out, really. Things are progressing well with Callie and well, I miss her when she's not with me. It's not that I don't love you, Cathy, just not in that way anymore. I hope you understand."

There are no words worth saying. No discussions to be had at all and no emotions other than relief, which surprises me. It's as if I can step out of my downtrodden skin like a butterfly from a chrysalis and as I gaze at my husband's familiar face, all I see is a stranger staring back at me.

So, with as much dignity as I can muster, I take a deep breath and say forcefully, "Get out."

His stunned expression almost makes me laugh before I hiss, "I would run if I were you because, well, I'm rather menopausal right now and liable not to be held accountable for my actions."

"What the..." Connor stares at me in complete shock as I point to the door and say with a low growl, "At least you have somewhere to go and just count yourself lucky that there's a bigger fool than me out there who is happy to deal with the shit that spouts from your mouth every time you open it. Don't bother to pack, I'll do it for you. Just take your miserable face somewhere else because I never want to see it again."

Connor makes to speak, and I yell, "Now, Connor! I don't want to hear it."

He scrapes back the chair and says angrily, "Fine. I'll go because you're being melodramatic as always. It's no wonder I fell out of love with you, if I ever did in the first place."

I watch my husband of over twenty-five years walk away as if he's a stranger. As the door bangs behind him, I sit for a considerable time trying to process the emotions that are racing through me right now. It's as if the door closed on my old life and I have yet to step through the next one. Moments like this don't come around very often, and I want to process this one before I move on. Connor is gone and I'm ecstatic to know I'm more than happy about that.

39
SAMANTHA

I am the weakest woman I know. Ben always did have the ability to charm me into agreeing to anything and last night was no exception. We had such a lovely time at the pub. It was almost as if the past few years never happened, and we were together again. He was charming, funny, and sweet, and I was surprised at how quickly we fell back into our usual routine.

Now, as I wake up beside him, I hate myself. I'm a fool and don't deserve to be happy. Who forgives their husband for cheating on them and running off with another woman as soon as they say sorry?

Me.

I do.

The weak, stupid fool who is obviously so desperate for attention, even his.

More than anything, I hate the way he looks so gorgeous, sleeping beside me as if I have woken from a bad dream, not reality.

The more I dwell on what happened after he left, the more I hate myself for letting him off so easily.

I suppose he caught me at a vulnerable moment, and I told myself he was leaving to go overseas, anyway. When he returns, I'll be living in Dubai, but he doesn't need to know that.

That knowledge makes me feel a lot better and so as he stirs, I say with a smile, "Morning."

He opens his eyes and stares into mine with a lazy grin that always did make my heart flutter.

"Morning gorgeous."

My heart thumps as his name for me reminds me when my life was perfect. At least I thought it was and as he reaches out and tucks my hair behind my ear, he whispers, "Thank you."

"What for?" I really hope he's not going to say for the sex because that would make me feel even worse, but he merely whispers, "For being you."

For some reason, it causes tears to fill my eyes, and he says softly, "Hey, don't cry. Please, I can't bear it."

I can't help it because why did he have to ruin such a good thing and what happened after was a direct result of it? I couldn't cope and I was vulnerable and let a predator in. I've had to live with that memory as well as the pain of losing the man I loved, and he doesn't even realise what he did.

I sit up and wrap my arms around my bended knees and sob gently as the past comes back to bite and then I am pulled against his muscular chest and rocked like a baby as he whispers, "It's ok, I've got you. Tell me what's bothering you and I swear I'll make it better."

I say nothing and he says with a slight shake to his voice, "Is it me? What I did to you? I'm so sorry, Sammy, I really am. I don't deserve to be here and if you say the word I'll leave but I'll never give up on us, please believe me because I've lost you once and I don't think I can stand losing you again. Unless..."

His words are like white noise swirling around me, and I shake my head against his chest and mumble, "It's not you."

"Then what? Who?" His arms tighten around me, and it's so good being in them. As if he can keep the world away, him included, and I'm telling myself this is for one moment in time. He leaves today and I will pick myself up and be the better woman. The one I should be who takes no shit, but I already realise I'm not. I'm weak and easily led, which is exactly what led me to this point.

I'm not sure how long we sit here for before he says gently, "I'm leaving today. I'm heading to the base where I'll be deployed. I haven't discovered where, but it's not a drill. However, I can't leave knowing you're upset. Whatever it is, please tell me. If it's me, I will do everything I can to make it up to you. If it's something else, I need to know so I can help you."

His words cause a fresh surge of tears and as I open my mouth, even I'm surprised at the words that come out.

"It's Daniel."

"Who?" He says in confusion, and I gulp, "Sonia's husband Daniel."

"What about him?" He sounds so confused and I drag in a deep breath and say with a wobble to my voice. "We were staying at a hotel in Suffolk for a few days and everyone was there, not long after you left."

He nods. "I remember the invitation."

"Well, I decided to go to take my mind off it all and yet when I saw how happy everyone was, it reminded me how unhappy I was."

He strokes my back like he would a pet dog and I snuggle into his chest, feeling empty inside.

"I went back to my room and Daniel was coming the other way. He must have seen I'd been crying because he stopped and asked what was wrong."

I gulp. "He was being so kind, and I never thought anything of it, but he took my arm and said he'd make sure I got back to my room."

Ben stiffens against me and his heart thumps against my cheek as I whisper, "As soon as I opened the door, he pushed it wide and stepped inside the room. I was a little surprised, but he said he was checking it was safe. He was being so kind I didn't say anything and watched as he opened the mini bar and poured us two vodkas. He told me it was to make everything better and like a fool, I believed him."

I brush my tears away and my voice shakes as I whisper, "He was being so kind, funny, and sweet. He tried to make me laugh, and it felt good. I even told him I was ok to go back to the others, but he grabbed my hand and told me we could have our own party."

A low growl rumbles against my ear and Ben's heart thumps even louder, but he says nothing, and I sob, "I told him to stop, Ben. I told him I didn't want to, but he carried on kissing me. He didn't stop there, and I tried so hard to fight him off, but he was too strong."

My tears splash against his skin as I unburden the darkest

secret in my soul and I cry, "He forced himself on me and I was too weak to stop him."

"He raped you." Ben's voice is calm, but he is anything but and I nod, saying in a whisper, "When he finished, he dressed and thanked me. He told me not to say anything because nobody would believe me, anyway. If Sonia found out, he would deny it and it would be his word against mine. I wanted him to leave so badly I agreed to get him to go. He reminded me that my friendship was at stake with the girls, and I should be flattered that he fancied me. Then he said casually that if I ever wanted a repeat performance, to call him. That now you had left, I could count on him to satisfy my needs."

Still, Ben says nothing and my voice shakes as I say pathetically. "I hate myself."

He shifts and pulls back, grasping my face in both hands, and stares deep into my eyes with a savage expression that terrifies me. His dark eyes are burning with fury as he hisses, "Never say that again. You are *not* to blame for any of it and if anyone is hating anyone around here, it's me. I hate what I did to you, and I hate what *he* did to you, but I promise you now, he will pay for what he did."

"No Ben. Forget I ever mentioned it."

I'm terrified as he growls, "Mentioned it. It's not a conversation you had that was told in confidence, Sammy. He raped you and tried to bully you into saying nothing."

"But it was years ago now. Leave it in the past where it belongs. I should never have told you."

I try to wrench away but he is too strong, and he says in a softer tone, "I love you, sweetheart. I always have and I am so thankful that you told me. I just want you to know that I am not taking anything for granted. I will call, write, and pester you until you fall in love with me again. I promise you that. If you don't want me, I will understand because I don't deserve you and probably never did."

He wipes away my tears with his thumbs and presses his lips to mine so gently it's a like a shot of the purest oxygen. As we share a gentle kiss, it chases away the madness and makes me feel better about my decision last night.

Past and present merge and have no place in my future. That part of my life is done, and I've had closure of sorts. Now I will move forward with none of the baggage of my past and who knows if I'll walk alone, or miracles can happen, and past mistakes can be forgiven and make us stronger in the future.

40

GINNY

My week with Omar was amazing. I never really expected we would connect as well as we did and I'm more surprised than anyone at how quickly I've fallen for him.

Despite my current situation, it's as if I don't have a care in the world and all because of him. He took my problem and said he would investigate, and I must believe in him and enjoy our time together. He wanted me to fall in love with him before he left for New York, and it didn't take me long to grant his request.

My only complaint is that I never met him sooner and his condition that I don't make any demands on him is fine by me. It appears that you can have it all because the past week has involved one hundred per cent of his attention and I've loved every minute of it.

I was sad to say goodbye when he left for his trip to New York, but he assured me he would be back in three weeks' time and to clear my diary. To be honest, I'm not sure how I'm feeling at the moment because if anything, it's as if I'm at his beck and call and yet he is such good company, why wouldn't I want to be available?

We have visited the opera, west end shows and eaten at the finest restaurants. He even booked a night in one of London's finest hotels and wined and dined me before presenting me with a Cartier bracelet. He is so generous and yet when I suggested meeting up with a few friends who invited me to a party, he turned down the invitation, saying that when we were together he didn't want to share my time.

It's obvious our relationship is strictly between the two of us, which worries me a lot because he could be hiding the biggest secret that will come back to bite me when I least expect it.

The day after Omar left, I am meeting Samantha in a bar by the river on the embankment. We've spoken on the phone, but this will be the first time we have met up since Dubai and I expect it's to discuss our move there.

It's a lovely Spring day when I head off to meet her, loving the crisp blue sky and the daffodils waving gently as I pass. Despite the cold, it's a glorious day and lifts my spirits.

She is already waiting as I edge inside the crowded bar and waves from her position by the window, jumping up to greet me when I reach the table.

"You look amazing, Ginny. What's your secret?"

I grin. "A good sex life starring the man from my dreams."

"Omar?" She raises her eyes in surprise and I nod smugly. "We spent the week together and now he's in New York on business."

"What was it like?" Her eyes are wide as she pours me a glass of wine from the bottle she pre-ordered and I sigh, causing her to grin.

"That good, huh?"

"Better."

She shakes her head and raises her glass to mine.

"I'm happy for you."

"So, tell me what you've been doing since we got home?"

I'm a little surprised when she blushes a colour that looks a lot like guilt.

"Sammy?"

I lean forward and note how she grips the stem of the glass a little tighter and laughs nervously.

"Well, I may have some news."

"What?"

"Ben."

My mouth drops to the floor as she stares at me anxiously.

"He left Kate."

"The woman he left you for and the mother of his children, Ben?"

I'm shocked and she nods, looking a little angry.

"As it turns out, they're not his children."

"Slow down." I hold up my hand and say in amazement. "You had better start at the beginning."

As she fills me in, I'm shocked because this is terrible. I can't believe what a mess it is, and hate that Samantha went through hell for nothing because a desperate woman stole her man and tricked him.

"So, what happens now?"

I'm a little cautious because he did cheat on her in the first place and I doubt I would be so forgiving and she sighs and glances out of the window before saying sadly, "I'm a fool, aren't I?"

"That depends on your answer."

"I haven't got one, really."

She looks back at me and smiles sadly. "Ben has returned to his job in active service. Nothing has changed, just the nature of our relationship. I no longer hate him, but I'm not sure if I want him back because it hurt so much the first time. What if it happens again?"

"It's too soon to know, I guess, and one night will hardly change your life. What do you *want* to happen is the more important question?"

She bites her bottom lip, meaning she's nervous, which also tells me her decision.

"I love him." She appears almost sad about that, and a surge of pity hits me.

Leaning forward, I smile and say reassuringly. "We can't help who we fall in love with, and that emotion has a habit of making our decisions for us. Take me, for instance. On paper, I am walking into a relationship as red flags line my route but I'm going there anyway because above everything else, I want to. I am even warning myself against Omar and yet find it easy to disregard my own advice because I want to go there, anyway. I'm guessing it's the same for you and Ben. What you had was special and one unfortunate action destroyed it. Does it have to be forever, though? There is no law against second chances, and you shouldn't beat yourself up over something that could be remarkable."

She almost looks relieved and smiles happily and pours some more wine into our glasses and raises hers in a toast.

"To two Summerhouse girls who make the wrong decisions and are loving every minute of it."

"To us."

It's so good to share this with Samantha. We are no different really and to any other person appear to be doing everything wrong. However, I know how good wrong tastes and there is nothing wrong with Mr Right.

As we drain the bottle and order another one, our conversation turns to our trip and I say with interest, "So, have you seen anyone else since you've been back?"

"No." She sighs. "I'm a little annoyed if I'm honest, though."

"Why?"

"Because Sonia isn't answering my texts or calls and still owes me five thousand pounds for her share of the bill."

"Five thousand pounds! Are you kidding me? My bill was only two hundred and thirty-five pounds. What the hell were they ordering, gold?"

I'm shocked, and Samantha nods miserably. "Apparently, they hadn't paid for their suite before they came and so that was included. Amanda booked ours separately because they were much cheaper. Then there were spa treatments and meals in the expensive restaurant. Bottles of prosecco and visits to the hotel patisserie."

"But that's, well, disgusting." I can't comprehend it, and Samantha nods. "The total was close to ten thousand pounds, but Amanda paid her share and Sonia still owes me hers but doesn't appear to be in a hurry to pay up."

"What are you going to do?" I can't imagine the nightmare that would spell for me and Samantha shrugs. "Hope that she settles it before the bill deadline. I mean, I could pay it, but I don't have much in the way of savings and it would almost wipe me out."

"Same." I feel sick when I think of my own predicament because if my mortgage payments increase, I won't have much left to live on and it brings me to ask, "What about your plan to live in Dubai? That could solve both our problems."

She seems worried. "I suppose, but now Ben is back in my thoughts, I'm wondering if I should change anything until I find out what's happening."

"But you said he was going away."

"To work but will be back on leave and he's asked if I'll meet him for a meal out. A sort of date, I suppose."

"Will you?" I already guess my answer from the worried frown on her face, but I note the deep yearning in her eyes. That look where you want something so much but know it's bad for you. We are so alike because I share that look and it strikes me that we are considering how it looks rather than how it feels. Is happiness hidden behind appearances? I'm guessing it is for most of us because we are humans who care a little too much about what other people think of us, even to the detriment of our own desires.

"I say go for it. With Ben, I mean." Even I'm surprised when the words come out of my mouth, and Samantha looks on in surprise. But her grateful smile makes it clear that I said the right thing.

"Do you think I should? I mean, you don't think badly of me for being so weak?"

"No. I don't."

I smile ruefully. "I know a lot about doing the wrong thing and sometimes the right thing is the least expected one."

Samantha nods and smiles with considerable relief and I say thoughtfully.

"I'm disappointed that we won't be beginning a new chapter together, but excited for the next one in my own story."

"Which is?"

She smiles with interest as I grin.

"Like you, I am going against popular opinion and doing what the hell suits me. If that means I'm 'available' whenever my sexy Arab is in town, then that's what I'm doing. If I get bored, or find I'm no longer happy with the situation, I may move on and try something else. Life has always been like that for me, and I suppose I'm too old to start changing."

"Then here's to the future."

Samantha raises her glass and smiles. "To doing the wrong thing and enjoying every sinful minute of it."

As we touch glasses, I wish her well. I wish us both well, but I don't wish Sonia and Daniel well. It appears that some friends take more than they give, and Sonia and Daniel may have taken a little too much and I wonder how long it will be before it all comes back to bite them.

41

SONIA

It's been six weeks since my trip to Dubai and life isn't getting any easier. If anything, it's even worse and I'm more worried than ever about my alcohol consumption.

Ever since Amanda and Jasper left, I've been waiting for the call telling us everything is ok, and we've survived another crisis.

I hate that Daniel is carrying on as if nothing has happened and his chirpiness is beginning to irritate me.

I wish we had no worries. It's been a constant theme throughout our marriage, and I'm tired of it. Daniel didn't really turn out to be the husband I thought he would be. He's arrogant, dismissive, and appalling at his job. If he was a good husband, I could forgive him that, but he's not. He always lurches from one big mistake to another, and I blame him for every crisis in my life because it's usually caused by him.

Then there are the affairs. The women from his office who throw pitying glances my way at work functions. The scent of perfume on his collar that overwhelms me when I tug his shirts from the laundry basket. A smattering of face powder or blusher, the stain a glaring admission of his guilt. The way he brings me flowers unexpectedly with a sheepish grin and a declaration of love, telling me he has something to feel guilty about.

Then there are the messages on his phone that I steal a glance at when he's in the shower. Declarations of love and plans to meet up.

I wonder if he's ever told them about me. That he has a wife who, for all intents and purposes, has done nothing wrong. I'm fed up with ignoring the practical part of my soul telling me to leave him. Divorce him and claim half of what we're worth, which, as it turns out, isn't a lot.

He re-mortgaged the house without telling me, and I wonder what else he's done in my name.

I hope this investment Jasper talked him into is worth it because increasingly I am coming to the conclusion that my marriage is in trouble, and I should cut my losses before my drinking gets out of hand and my health suffers. The fact I have two boys who idolise their father is a problem because if I left Daniel, they would come down firmly on his side. I'm not sure I'm prepared to be the outcast of the family and so I suffer in silence and wait for something to happen.

It does.

Six weeks after our trip to Dubai, to be precise, when I get a text from Amanda. That alone surprises me because since that night we have barely spoken, let alone text daily as we usually do.

Amanda is having a party for her own fiftieth and has invited all the usual suspects. I'm not sure how I feel about seeing them all again because Samantha must be pretty pissed off with me for not returning her calls regarding the money I owe her.

Then there's Ginny who has been rather frosty every time I've asked if she fancies meeting up. Catherine has also gone quiet on me and I expect it's because of the money Daniel lost them.

I'm not loving myself right now and only have myself to blame. When I think of the values, I live by, I wonder when they ruined my life. Wealth has become more important to me than friendship, and I'm not proud about that.

When I'm faced with the life Amanda lives, I recognise it's the one of my own dreams and I resent her for that. She has what I wanted all along, and I'm the fool who dropped it into her lap. The fact she's paid for it a thousand times over doesn't make the envy go away. I was always the one everyone looked up to and yet when Amanda joined our group, she became the centre of it. She has the biggest house, the best stories and a husband who made more money than all of us put together and who wouldn't be jealous of that? The fact she's such a nice person saved her because I did consider cutting her out of our group at one time. Then I would be the one everyone admired and envied. I have never liked being second best, but I am to her.

Now my own future depends on her and in my poisoned mind, part of me believes she owes me that.

So, I look forward to the party and hope that we can put this awkward period behind us when Jasper announces that the investment paid off and normal service will be resumed.

I dress for the occasion in a white dress with nude heels and a smart white jacket to keep off the chill. It will probably be heated to eighty degrees in their house but it's still cold in the evenings and knowing Amanda she has arranged a firework display to spell out her name with a big freaking love heart at the end, reminding the rest of us how much her husband loves her.

Well, lucky her because I doubt if mine knows what love is and so as we prepare to leave, I decide that tonight will be the one on which I alter my path in life. I will toast Amanda's birthday with a vow to change my own life because I don't like the old one, anyway.

Daniel is quiet on the drive over and I'm happy about that. After a while, he huffs and says in a whining voice, "I hope Jasper has some good news about the investment. I could certainly use some."

"Why?" My voice is as sharp as my mind because it's obvious Daniel is worried about something.

"I think you should know things aren't good at work."

He sighs heavily, and it reminds me that we've had this conversation before, several times over the years.

"You mean they're firing you?"

I'm blunt and he says angrily, "Thanks for your sympathy."

"That ran out years ago." I snap, weary as always when I prepare myself for change and to pick up the pieces yet again.

"It's worse than that."

"Worse than being fired." My voice shakes as he tells me

something new and he nods, his face ashen in the dusky light of the car.

"I'm being prosecuted."

"What for?"

I'm stunned and hope to hell it's for a speeding ticket, but he confirms my worst fears when he says in a strangely strangled voice. "For fraud."

For a moment, I let the news sink in and then say tentatively, "Maybe you should start from the beginning."

He says with an irritated sigh, "I wanted to save you from this, but it's likely to become common knowledge and you would hear it, anyway."

"And that's the only reason you're telling me?" I sound incredulous and he shrugs. "It's what I do, Sonia, what I've always done. Shield you from the harsh realities of life. Provide you with your happily ever after without knowing the hardship of earning it. Truthfully, you never have–earned it, I mean, and I'm the one who has bent over backwards to make you happy to the detriment of my own."

He sounds so aggrieved it fires something inside me and I say sharply, "You say I haven't earned it. I disagree. I've earned every penny of it because I married *you*. A man who cheats, lies, and then expects me to beg my friends to make it all go away, just to make you look as if you know what you're doing. You never have and this is just another example of that, so tell me, Daniel, what is it this time?"

I take deep calming breaths because my nerves are shot to pieces, and I am craving the delightful reassurance of alcohol right now.

Daniel says in a voice devoid of any emotion, "The Hades development."

"That again?"

I huff and he says irritably, "Yes, that again. It will never go away all the time the authorities investigate my part in it. You see, to invest, I needed to be separate from it."

"What are you talking about?" I snap and he yells, "For fuck's sake, Sonia, will you shut your mouth for one second and listen to me?"

It has the desired effect and I fall silent, more with shock than anything, because Daniel has never yelled at me like that and I'm shaking.

He snaps, "I started a company in your name."

This doesn't sound good, and a thousand questions are begging to be heard, but for some reason I hold them back as he continues.

"I set up a company called Summerhouse holdings. I re-mortgaged the house and used the money to invest in Hades. I also invested Connor and Ginny's money in Summerhouse holdings and named them as shareholders. That way, I could manage your investment without being named, and that is the part I'm being investigated for."

"I don't understand." I really don't and my head is spinning with this information. How the hell could he set up a company in my name without my knowledge and plough my friend's money into it? It doesn't make sense, and he says with a deep sigh.

"I've been found out and the authorities are looking into it. You will get a visit along with Ginny and Connor and so I need you to tell them you knew. Persuade the others to cover for me too, because that is the only way they will get their investment back."

"How will they get their investment back?" I'm pushing aside the sheer audacity of the man asking me to lie for him and to persuade my friends to do the same and he says with desperation, "I went to Jasper after our meal and told him I had already re-mortgaged the house and put the money into

Hades. He came up with a solution that made perfect sense and that is what I'm banking on pulling us through.

"What have you done, Daniel?" I sense a storm rushing towards me that I may not escape his time and his voice reaches me from hell itself as he growls, "I sold our house to him."

42

SONIA

"You did what?"

I can't believe what I'm hearing, and Daniel says scratchily, "It was the only way. He paid me the market value and used the money to invest in his new project. Think about it. When the investment is at its highest, we will treble our money to close on two million pounds."

His voice raises higher and the excitement in his voice is hard to ignore as he says with greedy glee. "We pay Jasper, the six hundred thousand we owe him. Then I pay Connor and Ginny the four hundred thousand they originally invested in Hades."

"Stop."

I cut him off and say slowly, "Surely, you mean you will pay them six hundred thousand if you treble their money.

All we would get is the money Jasper lent us back. We would pay off the mortgage and be no better off."

Daniel says with a slight edge to his voice, "The house is worth just over one million. We would have to sell up and downsize and release some equity to plough back into the business."

"What business?" I'm so confused, and he says as if talking to a two-year-old. "Summerhouse Holdings. With Jasper's help, we could invest in other projects and one day may even be able to buy a bigger house and replace our pension pot."

"What do you mean, replace?" There's an awkward silence as the penny drops and I say incredulously, "You robbed our pension too?"

My whole world explodes in one sensational moment of realisation and Daniel only confirms my worst fear when he says roughly, "Marriage to you doesn't come cheap, Sonia. Maybe you should start looking at your own part in this before judging me."

He turns into Amanda's private driveway, effectively ending this conversation and as we move slowly towards the house at the end, it reminds me that I've finally reached the dead end in my own marriage and just as soon as this nightmare is over, so is my marriage to Daniel.

———

We reach the house in silence, and I swear I'm having a panic attack as I step from our car and head towards the biggest house I have ever seen. Amanda's house. Bought and paid for with no mortgage attached. The triple garage is home to the newest cars, also bought and paid for. The pension pot is currently at the maximum donation level for each of them, ensuring their luxurious lifestyle continues well into their retirement thus enabling them to carry on enjoying amazing holidays that are paid for in full on a debit card. They have everything and we, as it turns out, have nothing and it's now obvious to me that we never have.

Ginny is the first person I see when we step inside as she shrugs out of her coat and turns to greet us.

I'm surprised when she pulls the stranger forward, she met in Dubai and says almost smugly, "Hi, Sonia, you remember Omar don't you?"

I nod, staring at him with envy because Ginny certainly hit the jackpot with him. He positively screams wealth from the gold Rolex on his wrist to his well-tailored suit. Even his teeth dazzle as he nods and turns with curiosity towards Daniel and glances at him with a strange expression on his face.

I swear my husband turns as white as milk as he stares at Omar, causing me to share a look with Ginny, who also appears to notice it.

Daniel looks at Omar as if he's seen a ghost and as Omar extends his hand, Daniel's lies limp inside it as they shake hands in an awkward moment.

Amanda breaks up the encounter by saying loudly, "Guys, it's so good to see you."

I turn my attention to her and smile, thrusting the flowers into her hand that I paid for with some money I found in the cookie jar, and she smiles. "They are lovely. Thank you so much."

Ginny hugs her and, reaching down, hands her a Harrods bag, saying apologetically, "I'm not sure if you have this already but they included a gift receipt so if you want to change it that will be fine by us."

"Us?" I stare in amazement as Omar steps beside Ginny and takes her hand, staring into her eyes with a blazing look that makes my legs tremble and it doesn't escape my attention that Ginny is wearing a sparking diamond on her engagement finger and I gasp, "Ginny are you…"

"Engaged." Her smile is as brilliant as the diamond that catches the light as she holds it aloft and she smiles happily, "Omar proposed when he returned from New York along with this Tiffany ring."

"You're getting married!" Amanda says excitedly and yet Ginny just shares an amused smile with Omar and grins.

"Not in the usual sense of the word, but we have come to an understanding. We are committed to one another, and the ring symbolises that, but we will never marry. Just enjoy the security the commitment brings."

I wonder if I should tell her that security is the last thing a marriage gives you and I steal a sly glance at my husband, who appears to want to be anywhere but here right now. Luckily, we are spared from saying anything when the door opens and Catherine heads inside, causing us all to do a double take.

Ginny whispers, "Wow, Connor's shaped up. I hardly recognise him."

She giggles as we stare at our friend who is holding the hand of a stranger and she approaches us, saying a little sheepishly, "Guys. Meet Jack, my, um, well, friend."

"With obvious benefits." Ginny whispers and yet I can't share the joke because what the hell is happening? It's as if nothing makes sense anymore.

Jack says with a friendly smile, "I'm pleased to meet you all."

I watch in disbelief as Catherine hands Amanda a bouquet and a brightly wrapped gift that reminds me of my own inability to buy her anything. I even considered wrapping up something of mine that I never used, but the fact she bought most of them is low, even for me. In fact, the more I consider our friendship over the years, the more I realise what a bitch I've been, and it's taken my current situation to teach me that I really don't like myself very much.

As I watch my friends fawning over Amanda, I finally understand why. It's not her money, her generosity, or her hospitality that makes them like her. It's her sweet personality. The way she always has a smile on her face and listens rather than talks. The sweet little gestures she makes when anyone is upset or sick. The way she celebrates their achievements and cries with them when they're hurting. It's not the money that makes them like her, it's because she is a bloody good friend.

As I stare at the scene in front of me, it's as if I'm on the edge looking in. The one on the outside because I jumped outside the circle when I lost the true meaning of friendship. It's not just our money we've lost, I can blame Daniel for that, but it's the humanity inside me that went years ago and forced me outside a place I should have clung onto with all my might.

The Summerhouse girls were fearless, and their greatest strength was their close bond. In this moment of realisation, it occurs to me that is the greatest failure of my life. Losing sight of that and believing that happiness lied in another direction entirely.

The door opens once again, bringing with it an icy chill that causes me to shiver inside. As I turn to see the addition to the party, it strikes me that we never made it out of the hallway. It's as if we choreographed our arrivals and so I'm not surprised to see Samantha enter with a loud, "When is it Spring? It's freezing out there."

I half turn and blink in astonishment when I see who has accompanied her.

Her errant husband Ben is holding her hand tightly and smiles as she says a loud, "Surprise!"

We all share a look and I notice the smirk on Ginny's face telling me she knew at least and I'm even more surprised when Ben steps forward and hugs Amanda, before saying apologetically, "Happy birthday, Amanda. Please accept my most sincere apologies for what I'm about to do."

I'm not sure if it's my overactive imagination or not, but I swear Daniel steps back as Ben turns and the glare he directs at my husband would burn ice.

In two strides he reaches him, and I scream as he punches Daniel square in the face and as Daniel yells and falls to the ground, Ben aims a hard kick in his ribcage as Samantha screams, "Ben! No!"

The thing that amazes me most of all is the silence. Everybody stares at my wailing husband on the ground, and it's as if my life is moving in slow motion. The faces spin around me as I struggle to understand what's happening and as Ben steps back, he growls, "That's for raping my wife."

The collective gasp hits the room like a Mexican wave as Samantha's sobs echo through my brain.

Rape. That word is the loudest one I hear, causing me to say with a stutter, "But you said…"

I stare at Daniel, a pitiful figure on the ground as he lies bleeding in a crumpled heap and I turn to Samantha and say in shock, "Is this true? Did Daniel rape you?"

Her misery is palpable as she sobs, "Yes."

I say in confusion, "But he told me you threw yourself at him and begged him to sleep with you."

The others gasp as they look between us, and I turn to my husband and yell. "You lied to me!"

He says nothing, which tells me everything and with a well-aimed kick, I catch him square in the ribs and hiss, "You bastard. You fucking deranged bastard."

As I turn to face Samantha, no words can describe how bad I feel and I shake my head in disbelief and say, "I'm so sorry."

"It's not your fault." Samantha tries to smile through her tears, and I can't help myself and surge towards her, my arms outstretched as I clasp her close to my chest and break down in her arms. It's as if all the trauma, the years of pretending and the glass wall I have built around my emotions are destroyed in one huge earthquake as everything I have struggled to keep in place falls at my feet.

I loathe myself even as much as I hate my husband, because what was I thinking? I am a monster, and I don't like how that feels.

43
AMANDA

Of everything that happened tonight, watching Sonia break down is the most shocking. I've never seen her show emotion in all the time I've known her. She is the strong one. The woman who shores up our foundations, and it's hard to watch. I'm surprised that I still care and yet relieved to discover I do. Despite everything, there is still a huge part of me that loves this woman and so I step forward and say firmly, "Come on, Sonia. Let's get you sorted."

She allows me to drag her away and my heart lifts when the rest of our friends join us as we head upstairs to my bedroom.

As we surge inside, Ginny says kindly, "It's ok, Sonia. You have us. We're going nowhere."

Sonia lifts her tear-streaked face to us and says in a trembling voice, "Why?"

We say nothing and her voice breaks as she says with a sob, "Why do you even try with me? I'm a monster and I married an even bigger one."

Samantha says sadly, "Because none of us are perfect."

We stare at her as she sits on the bed and stares around the group.

"I should have admitted what happened, but I was so scared of losing your friendship. Daniel told me that nobody would believe me and so I kept quiet through guilt that I'd led him on somehow."

I feel so bad for her and sit beside her on the bed, placing my arm around her.

I'm shocked when Sonia sits on the other side and does the same and Ginny says angrily, "Men are fucking bastards. Except Omar, of course."

For some reason, that makes us all laugh out loud, which does a very good job of lightening the atmosphere.

Catherine says softly, "I'm divorcing Connor."

Ginny retorts, "I wondered about his replacement. Who is he? He seems nice."

"He is."

Catherine fills us in, and we stare at her in shock.

Ginny says with a whistle, "Good for you and what a bastard. Connor, I mean."

Samantha says sadly. "I know how that feels. I'm sorry Cathy."

"So, why is Ben with you?" Cathy interrupts and Samantha tells us her story with a shaky smile. "Do you think

I'm weak for taking him back?" She says, directing her question to the room and we all say as one, "No!"

Ginny says quickly, "I would think less of you if you allowed other people's opinions to shape your decision. If I've learned one thing in life, it's that you should always do what makes you happy."

"You've never strayed from that path, Ginny." Cathy grins, causing us all to laugh out loud because Ginny has always done what the hell she likes and always has.

Sonia says in a small voice. "I'm sorry girls."

"What for?" I say kindly because even though the list is long, I don't really want her to admit to it.

"For being a shit friend, I suppose. For always believing I was above you and expecting you to be grateful for that. I'll try to be better."

Nobody says anything because what would we say, anyway? We all know she's right and I'm just grateful Sonia realises that at long last.

Sensing the mood has lightened, I say with a smile, "Come on. We have a party to attend."

As we all head back to it, I wonder if Sonia will be strong enough for the rest of the surprises that are yet to reveal themselves.

―――

We find the men in the living room, huddled around talking. Daniel is sitting on the sofa, his head in his hands. He is holding his nose with a clutch of tissues and even though he strikes a forlorn figure, I have no sympathy for him.

I follow the men's lead and completely ignore him and say loudly, "Jasper, maybe we should fetch some drinks."

He nods and as we leave the room, I whisper, "That was awful. I feel so bad."

"Why?" Jasper shrugs. "They deserved it."

"I know, but for some reason, seeing Sonia break down wasn't pleasant to watch."

To my surprise, he stops and pulls me into his arms and leaning down, kisses me so sweetly it makes my heart beat faster. As he pulls back, I smile and say softly, "What was that for?"

"For being you, Amanda. For being a good friend and the most amazing wife and mother. I certainly hit the jackpot with you, and I will spend the rest of my life making it up to you."

"You owe me nothing." I say emphatically, and he smiles.

"I owe you everything. You allowed me to be selfish. To pursue my dream and cut you out. To put work before family just to inflate our bank account and for what? To keep adding more and more until I lost sight of what was important."

I'm shocked as Jasper opens his heart to me for the first time.

He shakes his head. "The reason I retired was because three of my colleagues died in as many months. Heart attacks brought on by stress, according to the doctors."

I gasp as he says bitterly. "They worked so hard and for what? They never got to enjoy the money they made and left their families without a husband and father. I don't want to be that corpse, Amanda. I want us to start living and enjoying the reason that kept us apart. I love you and I never told you that enough. Possibly not for a few years when I should have told you every day of our life together. You are the most precious thing in my life, along with our children, and I just want you to know that."

As we share a moment, possibly the sweetest one of our

marriage, I congratulate myself on meeting my soul mate and sticking it out. He became a stranger, but he came back to me in the end and now we can start over–together.

Two hours later and the moment I have been both dreading and anticipating with a building excitement reaches us as Jasper clears his throat and says with a loud, "Can I have your attention please?"

The room falls silent as he turns to me and says fondly, "Happy birthday to the best wife a man could ever wish for. To Amanda."

As our friends echo his words, I stare around with a smile of happiness that hasn't been there for some time. Finally, everything is right in my world which almost makes me stop him here, but it's not just me this concerns. It's for my friends, so my heart lurches when he says loudly, "I have news as it happens."

He glances at the dejected figure of Daniel, who hasn't moved from the sofa and says loudly, "Daniel came to me for help with the Hades project, which I'm afraid I had no control over. The money you all invested was lost when the shares collapsed."

I register the pain on Ginny and Catherine's faces and note that Julie stiffens and glances at Daniel with a sharp look of blame.

"I told him of another investment that had come to my attention which could be worth looking into. However, it required investing even more money, so Daniel agreed to sell his house to me in order to get your money back."

Even though this isn't strictly true, I experience a surge of love for my husband because he is giving Daniel way more credit than he deserves and he continues, "The plan was to invest the money in the company and when the shares doubled, to sell and pay everyone back their money."

Ginny glances at Catherine and they share an excited smile, and I am happy they won't be out of pocket.

Jasper continues. "I set the ball rolling and watched the shares grow in price. They were building nicely, which was probably because of the investment we made. Then I got a call that changed everything."

I note Daniel's anxious expression as we all stare at Jasper, wondering what has gone wrong now, and he says with a sigh. "The owner of the company I'd lined up to buy the business called me with bad news. The current owner had sold up, lock stock and barrel and the new owner bought most of the shares. The markets got nervous, and the share price started falling, so I had no choice and sold. They were snapped up by the new owner, who now owns the entire company."

Daniel turns even whiter, if that's possible, and Jasper shakes his head.

"Although we never lost money, we never reached our goal, so the original investment hasn't grown as much as I hoped it would."

Sonia glares at Daniel as Jasper turns to my friends. "Ginny, both you and Connor will get your original investment back. I'm sorry it isn't more but at least you will break even."

"Oh, thank God." Ginny says with considerable relief, and I note Omar reach for her hand and squeeze it in a show of affection that makes my own heart flutter. This has been a long time coming and I'm happy for them.

Catherine says gratefully, "Thank you. I'll let Connor

know and we can add it to the divorce settlement that the lawyers are currently working on."

It strikes me that despite the fact she is going through a nasty divorce, she has never looked so happy.

Then Jasper turns to Samantha and says with a smile. "I understand Sonia owed you five thousand pounds from your trip. I'm sure she won't mind if I pay you back on their behalf out of the profits."

He checks with Sonia, who just nods with a sad smile. "Of course. I'm so sorry, Sammy. I've been swerving your calls because I couldn't admit to you that I didn't have the money to pay you back."

"It's fine, Sonia, really it is." Samantha says sweetly and Daniel says roughly, "So what are you saying, Jasper? What about us?"

Jasper's tone changes and he says with distaste, "Your investment was four hundred thousand pounds after you paid off the mortgage on your home. I made up the shortfall and in total we invested one million pounds. We made one million, two hundred thousand, which isn't a bad return for six weeks' work. I'm sure you will agree."

"But you said it would treble." Daniel yells, but Jasper merely shrugs.

"It would have done if the other company hasn't stepped in. As it did, this is the breakdown of your investment. You sold your home to me for one million pounds, of which four hundred thousand was left when the mortgage was paid off. As I said I made up the rest and bought one million pounds worth of shares."

The room is silent as we stare at Jasper doing what he does best as he rattles off figures as if it's Monopoly money.

"In total we made one million, two hundred thousand when we sold our shares. Six hundred thousand paid my investment back. Four hundred and five thousand pays Ginny, Connor and Samantha back. This will work in your favour if you are investigated regarding the Hades consortium and Summerhouse Holdings, leaving a profit of one hundred and ninety-five thousand. Deduct the money you owe us that has built up over the past thirty years, which totals ninety-five thousand, it leaves you with a profit of one hundred thousand pounds."

Sonia looks between Jasper and Daniel and voices what the rest of us are thinking. "I don't understand. What's happening?"

Jasper says kindly. "I propose having a sixty per cent share in Summerhouse Holdings in lieu of the money I invested on your behalf. In effect, buy into your company and become the majority shareholder, effectively taking over the running of the company."

Sonia shakes her head. "How does this affect us?"

Jasper says slowly. "Rather than sell your home to pay me back, its best if you retain the forty per cent share courtesy of the four hundred thousand equity in your home. I am happy to leave it as a property investment and will have a contract drawn up that you, as a company director, can live there for a token sum until you get back on your feet."

I swear you could hear a pin drop in the room as everyone stares at Daniel, who suddenly erupts like a bubbling volcano. "One hundred thousand! You are joking."

"And an asset worth one million pounds in the company your wife is a director of. Excuse me for mentioning this, Daniel, but you should count yourself lucky because you have secured your family's future."

Daniel stares at him as if he has a thousand thoughts running through his mind and then he slumps on the sofa and says in a strained voice, "I suppose I should thank you."

Sonia stands up and says loudly, "Of course you should thank him. He's given us our life back. He could have insisted we sell the house and there is nothing you could do about that. Then where would we be?"

She turns to Jasper and her eyes shine with gratitude as she says softly, "Thank you."

Jasper smiles and catches my eye before he says softly, "Thank Amanda. She only wanted the money you borrowed from everyone paid back, with minimum cost to you. Nobody wants to see you with nothing. We are all friends here and we are happy to welcome new ones."

To my surprise, he turns to Omar and chuckles softly. "Although I never expected you to walk into my home tonight."

Omar shrugs. "A happy coincidence."

Every pair of eyes in the room turns their curious gaze to Omar, even Ginny as Jasper says, "Daniel recognised you almost as quickly as I did."

He says to the room. "Omar is one of my clients. I manage several funds for him and his associates, and I believe Daniel has also come across him."

Omar nods. "Our paths have crossed only once."

I swear Daniel tries to make himself invisible as Omar says in his deep voice, "Daniel cost my associates rather a lot of money and we withdrew our account. He lost his job for that."

Sonia snaps, "Why am I not surprised?"

Jasper shakes his head. "Omar heads up a consortium of some of the wealthiest men on the planet. He manages their investment portfolios and is probably the most sought-after investor in the world right now. He plays the markets and utilises the best each country has to offer to make them even more money. They were behind the acquisition of our investment and represent the company who now owns the company we invested in."

We all stare at Omar, who merely shrugs and turns to Ginny, who is gazing at him in stunned disbelief, and he smiles gently. "It's why I'm so busy, my darling. When you told me what had happened to you, I investigated and discovered you never invested in the Hades consortium. You invested in Summerhouse Holdings and when I learned of Jasper's plan, I stepped in to make sure you didn't lose out a second time."

Ginny says with confusion. "I don't understand."

Omar smiles gently, "Jasper told me about the investment in one of our routine meetings and mentioned the name of the company he was representing. I knew it was the same one, and I decided not to leave anything to chance. I needed to guarantee you would get your money back because your happiness is important to me, and it made me realise that this may be my life, but it's not everything. Now I have someone to share it with, even though I can't pretend I'll be the most reliable date ever."

Ginny shakes her head and smiles. "This is perfect. You must do what's right for you and I'll do me."

"That's Ginny." Catherine laughs and the rest of us follow because if there was ever a match made in heaven, it's theirs.

EPILOGUE
SONIA

SIX MONTHS LATER

Not long after Amanda's party, Daniel was arrested for fraud and fired from his job and subsequent investigations revealed he had acted fraudulently, not just with Summerhouse Holdings but also with several other accounts.

I was investigated and when it became apparent that none of us named in the company knew anything about it, Daniel was arrested for fraud and after a long trial, was sent to prison for seven years.

Luckily, we still have somewhere to live thanks to Jasper and, as a director in the company, he assures me that I will have enough to live on and I'll be eternally grateful for that.

He told me he was happy to have something to do in his retirement, although Amanda may not share his enthusiasm while he builds Summerhouse Holdings into an asset that will benefit us all.

I finally stepped up and went back to work. It's not much,

just a few shifts in a dress shop in town, but it makes me feel as if I'm doing my bit to help. I'm enjoying the experience. It gives me more to think about than myself and diverts my mind from the nightmare my life is right now.

The boys are angry at their father and really stepped up, telling me that family means more than money and will every single time.

Then, two weeks ago, the police paid us another visit and this time they came with devastating news.

Daniel had hung himself in his cell one night, leaving a suicide note that will live with me forever.

Sonia

I can't carry on. I'm taking the coward's way out because I've lost everything. My dignity, my self-respect, and my livelihood. I can't live knowing what a failure I am, but I want you to know I did it all for you. When we first met, I read your diary and one particular entry influenced everything I've ever done.

When I grow up, I only want to marry a man with money because that is the only thing that will make me happy.

I'm sorry I couldn't fulfil your dreams my darling, but I tried. I tried so damned hard it killed me in the end. Everything I did was to make that dream come true because you are my dream come true. I considered the affairs with other women as my weakness, my punishment because I never believed I was good enough for you. I was right. You deserve so much more. A man like Jasper. That is what I tried to be, but failed. So, I'm bailing out the coward's way. Tell the boys I love them and not to think badly of me, but I can't bear to see the disappointment on their faces. My family is and always will be everything to me, and I did it all for you.

Thank you for making my dreams come true. I hope that one day you find a man who can succeed where I failed. I love you. Goodbye, my forever love.

Your loving husband
Daniel xx

As I watch my sons pay their last respects to the man they idolised, my heart is so heavy it almost drags me down. If anyone failed, it was me. I demanded something he was incapable of giving and it's my fault he's lying cold in the ground.

I shiver as the chill from the wind catches me and as my sons step back, they each take one of my hands and squeeze them gently. They don't blame me; they don't even blame Daniel.

They are the lucky ones.

As we turn and walk away from a wasted life, I see my friends waiting, emotion showing on their faces as they witness a terrible ending to a sad story. Despite everything, I smile at them and am blessed they are here at all. I don't deserve them, and I don't deserve my sons, but I sure as hell deserve a second chance to make it up to them. To be a better person and learn what really matters in life. Friendship and family because if you have them, you are the wealthiest person in the world.

If you enjoyed this story you may be interested in Living The Dream

*Thank you for reading The Summerhouse Girls.
If you have enjoyed the story, I would be so grateful if you could post a review on Amazon. It really helps other readers when deciding what to read and means everything to the Author who wrote it.*

NB: This book is written in UK English

Connect with me on Facebook

Check out my website

Thank you

MORE BOOKS & ME

I feel very fortunate that my stories continue to delight my readers. The Girl on Gander Green Lane reached the number 1 spot in Australia in the entire Kindle Store. The Husband Thief and The Woman who Destroyed Christmas reached the top 100 in Canada, the UK and Australia.

I couldn't do it without your support, and I thank every one of you who has supported me.

For those of you who don't know, I also write under another name.

S J Crabb.

You will find my books at sjcrabb.com where they all live side by side.

As an Independent Author I take huge pride in my business and if anything, it shows what one individual can achieve if they work hard enough.

I will continue to write stories that I hope you will enjoy, so make sure to follow me on Amazon, or sign up to my Newsletter, or like my Facebook page, so you are informed of any new releases.

With lots of love and thanks.

Sharon xx

(M J Hardy)

Ps: M J Hardy is a mash up of my grandmother's names. Mary Jane Crockett & Vera Hardy. I miss you both so much & wish you knew this chapter in my life. One of my fondest memories is sitting in my grandmother's rocking chair by her gas fire, reading her collection of Mills & Boon books when I was about 12 years old. I wonder what she thought of that – I dread to think!

Check out my other books

The Girl on Gander Green Lane

The Husband Thief

Living the Dream

The Woman who Destroyed Christmas

The Grey Woman

Behind the Pretty Pink Door

The Resort

Private Island

You're Invited!

Join my Newsletter

Follow me on Facebook

Printed in Great Britain
by Amazon